‖ ‖ ‖‖‖‖‖‖ ‖ ‖ ‖ ‖‖‖‖‖‖‖‖‖ ‖ ‖‖
W9-AAW-777

Praise for Nicholas Mosley

"One of the most compelling writers in the English language."
—Joyce Carol Oates

"[A] first-rate experimental novelist. . . . In an age of so much successful 'light fiction,' he's a special taste, the kind of writer whose books stick in your mind for weeks after you've finished them."
—*San Francisco Chronicle*

"When unmistakably brilliant writing is combined with natural insight, the result is likely to be most impressive. Nicholas Mosley writes realistically, with an admirable craft and surging talent."
—*New York Times*

"Nicholas Mosley, in a country never generous to experimental writing, is one of the most significant instances we have that it can still, brilliantly, be done."
—Malcolm Bradbury, *Vogue*

"A modernist mastodon whose project for fiction surpasses in grandiosity that of any American writer I know."
—Tom LeClair, *Washington Post*

"Mosley is that rare bird: an English writer whose imagination is genuinely inspired by intellectual conundrums."
—Robert Nye, *Guardian*

"Mosley is ingenious and cunning. . . . Anybody who is serious about the state of English fiction should applaud Nicholas Mosley's audacity—his skill is unquestionable."
—Frank Rudman, *Spectator*

Other Works by **Nicholas Mosley**

Fiction

Accident
Assassins
Catastrophe Practice
Children of Darkness and Light
Corruption
The Hesperides Tree
Hopeful Monsters
Imago Bird
Impossible Object
Inventing God
Judith
Meeting Place
Natalie Natalia
The Rainbearers
Serpent
Spaces of the Dark

Nonfiction

African Switchback
The Assassination of Trotsky
Beyond the Pale
Efforts at Truth
Experience and Religion
Julian Grenfell
The Life of Raymond Raynes
Rules of the Game
The Uses of Slime Mould: Essays of Four Decades

Look at the Dark

Nicholas Mosley

Dalkey Archive Press
Normal · London

Originally published in the United Kingdom by Secker and Warburg, 2005
Copyright © 2005 by Nicholas Mosley

First U.S. edition, 2006
All rights reserved

Library of Congress Cataloging-in-Publication Data available.
ISBN: 1-56478-407-X

Partially funded by a grant from the Illinois Arts Council, a state agency.

Dalkey Archive Press is a nonprofit organization located at
Milner Library (Illinois State University) and distributed in the UK
by Turnaround Publisher Services Ltd. (London).

www.dalkeyarchive.com

Printed on permanent/durable acid-free paper and bound in the
United States of America.

To Shiva Rahbaran

On a dark night a person searches on the brightly lit ground under a lamp-post. A passer-by asks – For what are you searching? The person says – For the keys to my house. The passer-by says – Is this where you lost them? The person says – No I lost them in the dark, but this is where the light is.

Look at the Dark

1

There was a time when I was drawn to the Hindu idea that in old age a man should hand over earthly power and possessions to younger members of his family; that he should leave home equipped with little more than a begging bowl and go out onto the highways and byways to watch the world go by. By thus casting off mundane attachments he might gain spiritual power; which at the approach of death should be of more use to him anyway. This was an acceptable image in the setting of India – the vegetation at the side of the road, the warmth of the setting sun, a few sacred cows to keep him company. And with the hope of enlightenment hovering about his head like a bird ready to peck out dross, excrescence, illusion.

But as the time approached at which I could reasonably call myself retired I had a comfortable home in London, a second wife considerably younger than myself who would look after me if I became ill, and an income from investments augmented by occasional fees from radio talks and television. And in England the climate was neither literally nor metaphorically conducive to old men wandering out onto highways and byways; it was cold, and there were enough people both old and young nowadays with begging bowls in doorways looking less for enlightenment than for funding for addiction.

And anyway, what was gained by a contemplation of the everyday world? There was beauty; but what was striking were the activities of humans which made it ugly. A more profitable exercise might be the Christian recommendation that before death one should look into oneself to assess the story of one's own follies and misdemeanours, with the chance that by acknowledging these one might become at peace with one's achievements.

In practice, I seemed to use all this as an excuse to watch more television. If modern conditions made going out on the road pointless, did not modern technology now bring highways and byways to oneself? And from the comfort of my chair, might I not try to make sense of self-reflections?

My wife Valentina would come in from work in the evenings and find me watching a news or current affairs programme which dwelt reverentially on stories of tragedy and squalor in various parts of the world: or maybe I would have become hooked on some grim quiz or a chat show in which participants seemed to delight in bringing humiliation on themselves. Valentina would say, 'Why do you watch this stuff?'

I would say, 'You and I know so little of the outside world. We live in an ivory tower.'

'You think that by this you'll gain enlightenment?'

'We should know about the dark.'

I might have elaborated – If humans can see how awful they are, there might be a chance of their making things better. But by this time Valentina was likely to be halfway out of the room, having heard so often my pontifications.

My wife Valentina was a psychotherapist. She went out each day to run groups for the sick and disturbed in hospitals and clinics, and was visited at home by students. She would say – I agree that one can come to terms with ordinary human misery.

In the main part of my own working life I had been an anthropologist with a special interest in language and literature. I had taught, lectured, written articles and books, about ways in which people and groups acted and interacted: about their efforts and their reluctance to understand these. Myself and my colleagues picked examples from limitless data; we formed theories of cause and effect; we fashioned patterns from material that might otherwise seem anarchic. Few of us claimed to be looking for objective truth: we judged the merits of claims and hypotheses on the grounds of consistency. We recognised – or some of us did – that to a large extent we were arranging things according to our own instincts and inclinations. But I could reassure myself that there was still some objectivity in acknowledging this: academic practice was an ongoing game in which players could feel that their work had value so long as its rules were obeyed – the rules being to keep discussion going rationally even if conclusions reached were at loggerheads.

But then in the second half of my life I had rebelled against this acceptance: I had felt that there was a 'truth' to be sought beyond the circumscription of games, however difficult this might be to define or to pursue in practice.

The setting to which I planned to retire in old age was the basement of the house in which Valentina and I lived in north London. Here there was a room where I worked (I had given up teaching; I had hoped to write one more book). Also in the basement were a bathroom and a small kitchen by means of which I could be largely self-sufficient. This was a help both to marriage, and to whatever path of understanding that I imagined I might take. And as age had rendered me more sleepless I had come to spend nights as well as days in this basement; Valentina could thus carry on unencumbered her busy life upstairs. We came together for supper, and some-times to watch television in the evenings. But I had come to like watching some programmes with the sound turned off; I felt that by standing back and watching the cavortings of the world without the distractions of speech or music, one might glimpse better what might be at the back of what appeared so crazy. But Valentina would say 'How can you know what people are up to if their words are separated from their actions?'

I would say 'It seems to me that people's words hardly ever have much to do with their actions. And there might be a way of understanding this.'

'But it's through spotting people's lies and cover-ups that one can get at truth.'

'One might get at it quicker by concentrating on what happens.'

One of the theories I had elaborated in my work was that although it was evident that language was the chief faculty that distinguished humans from animals, it could be seen as a curse as well as a boon, because it was so often used as a tool for deceit in humans' dealings with one another. Language was used to attack, to justify, to charm, to defend; it was seldom concerned with simply imparting information. In the as-it-were naked instincts of animals there was a straight-forwardness, however cruel. Humans had covered these with garments of manipulation that gave the appearance of decency, but were often no less cruel. This had been one of the themes, presumably, in the myth of the Tower of Babel; in which humans had been hoping to get to heaven by means of speech, and then had been prevented from so doing by being given discordant voices.

I had once asked a theologian – Why didn't God want humans to get to heaven? He had said – Because they were supposed to sort things out on earth.

4

This was one of those enigmatic pronouncements by which religious people seemed to dodge tricky questions; but which later I came to recognise as a not improper use of language.

It was when in my work I had become increasingly impatient with people who made a living out of using the hubbub of Babel – politicians, journalists, fellow academics – who used confrontation and argument like a game of skittles, depending on ideas being set up and knocked down, and then set up again, so that the game could go on—

—and on and on—

—it was through my growing hostility to this process that in later life I had looked for some philosophy other than Hindu or Buddhist stoicism or Christian preparation for another world, and had come across a form of Middle-eastern gnosticism which took for granted that the power-mechanisms of this world were absurd, but suggested that with part of oneself one could stand to one side of them as it were, not renouncing the world but moving to some extent in parallel to it, though not in such a way as to hope for one's own worldly power. But by interacting with it – by taking note of what nudged one or what one bumped into; by sticking one's neck out or even by making a bit of a fool of oneself from time to time – one might find oneself in some sort of partnership with the world, even with whatever in spite of apparent odds did in fact keep it going; whatever was responsible for order and wonder as well as lunacy and fear.

It was at this time that I had begun to be in some demand as a pundit on television, so that there I could ride forth on my hobby-horses with at least the chance of feeling I was not prancing on empty air. I would declare – It is absurd to think that by means of rational language one can discover or state 'truth': rational language is used to present a case like a lawyer; this can be countered validly by another rational case presented by another lawyer; and so on and so on. By way of illustration I would briefly argue the case for instance both for and against sending troops into Kosovo; both for and against American imperialism. I would try to remember to add – Language of course has an unequivocal validity if it is fashioned into art. And if I was accused of sitting on fences I would say – Yes, so that it may be easier for people to climb over them.

Valentina would say 'That's your use of language as art?'

'Yes.'

'But don't you see you're in danger of becoming a licensed clown?'

'Yes.'

'And that's what you want?'

'It's a reputable job.'

But after a time I was becoming dissatisfied with being typecast as even a jolly *agent provocateur*, and I was looking for a chance perhaps to go over the top and get out. It was after one such programme in which I had said that Americans needed terrorists for the sake of their sense of identity just as terrorists needed America for the sake of theirs, that I found that an invitation had already been sent to me for a series of appearances on American television. I thought – Well of course I must go: I can make some conclusive splash like Salome in front of King Herod, and then the FBI can come and crush me with their shields.

Valentina said 'You'll be as much use as a suicide bomber.'

I said 'Do you think Jesus was a suicide bomber?'

'No. Most likely they'll nobble you by offering you a Hollywood contract.'

'Which of course I'll accept.'

'I'm suspicious about your wanting to go to New York. I think you've got something up your sleeve.'

'Like a Fifth Avenue bathhouse.'

'I don't know about bathhouses.'

6

'At least they're politically correct.'

As it happened I did have what might be called a hidden agenda in wanting to go to New York, which was that my first wife Valerie might be there. (Valerie and then Valentina: might there have been some riddling agenda here?) Valerie and I had married when we were young; we had remained married with some success for many years; then we had drifted apart and had divorced after I had met Valentina. Valerie was a painter; she liked to have a life of her own: I had had my preoccupations. With some innocence we had tried to combine fidelity with freedom, and for a time this had seemed possible. Then reality or unreality had broken in; I had behaved outlandishly; there had been sadness but not too much acrimony. Valerie had gone to live in California, where she had been making a name for herself as a painter and was said to have a rich patron or lover. After a time we had seemed to be on quite reasonable if distant terms again.

There had been infidelity – but to what, as distinct from to whom?

I had wondered – Is it possible to understand a relationship more clearly after divorce than during a marriage? And in old age, should one not try to look at this?

It was from our son Adam that I had heard that Valerie might now be in New York. Adam when young had moved between us with apparent amicability. When I had been offered the chance to go to New York I had wondered if I should tell Valentina that Valerie might be there, but would not this be gratuitously asking for trouble? And would not any rapprochement with Valerie be a betrayal of Valentina? But this was the sort of argumentation that I thought should be given up and left to chance. And what were the odds against bumping into Valerie in New York?

In my memory I had behaved badly to Valerie; but how did she now see this? One of my hobby-horses was to suggest

7

that some people needed to feel guilty for a sense of identity just as others needed to feel they were always right. So should not efforts be made to straighten things out with Valerie? Or was this self-indulgence—

—But what was wrong with self-indulgence? And so on and so on.

I had once argued in a television programme – Even if two people are divorced is not the nature of a marriage such that they are always in some sense connected – like those particles one is told about at opposite ends of the universe.

My theologian friend had said – A state of grace is just the recognition that whatever happens is all right.

It was with this sort of stuff floating in my mind that I travelled to New York. This was a year or so after the destruction of the Twin Towers, and although there had been for a time some public self-questioning, Americans were overwhelmingly demanding that there should be retaliation. By the time I arrived in New York Afghanistan had been bombed and it seemed that plans were under way to invade Iraq – though it was not clear how this was relevant. A large number of suspected terrorists were being incarcerated without trial in a base in Cuba on the grounds that this was necessary for justice and freedom. I thought – If on my first television appearance I make sufficiently politically objectionable remarks, will there not indeed be a chance that I might be eliminated by the FBI or CIA without my having to worry about style of retirement? And would it not then be in order for me to say goodbye to Valerie in New York – especially as I do not even know her number.

On arrival I lay on my bed in the rather grand hotel at which my expenses were being paid and for once I did not want to start watching television. So should I not be out on the highways and byways where there might at least be the chance of bumping into Valerie—

Or should I be planning how to make such a splash-down on my first American television appearance that nothing else would matter.

What about – Of course the FBI do not want to discover actual bombers! They want to feel free to lock up anyone they choose.

Or – Of course suicide bombers are the most disliked sort of terrorists, because then there are no defendants from whom lawyers can get fat fees.

Or as a coup de grâce – You people need to have tragedy and terror in order to bring some intensity into the vacuity of your lives.

Before I had left London Valentina had said 'Perhaps I should come with you to New York to keep an eye on you.'

I had said 'But I don't think all jokers are in despair.'

In the evening of my first day in New York I went out walking in the streets. I had always been excited by the air of risk, of challenge, in New York, but now more than ever there was the impression that tall towers might fall and crush one; bodies holding hands come tumbling like confetti. Perhaps it was these intimations of catastrophe that were making me think once again of what a person should be concentrating on towards the end of his life – if not Hindu or Buddhist renunciation nor Christian repentance, then perhaps an attempt to gather memories and impressions as they floated and eddied in one's mind and to try with these to make sense of one's life – not so much understand it as to give it a form perhaps as in an artwork. For this after all is what humans can do: and what better indeed can they do for the world – not only in practice but in their minds, which might or might not be of the same stuff as the universe. And then the chaos, the meaningless, could go their own way; and the work, the seeds of complex order, would remain in operation. It was all this perhaps that was

9

now making me look back to the beginning of my marriage to Valerie.

On our honeymoon Valerie and I had gone to Africa and Valerie had had to go into hospital for an emergency operation; and I had become involved in an incident that even now I did not seem able to think about clearly: it was this that I wished to put before Valerie. Or would I rather just continue with my jokes about the world's absurd obsession with conspiracies, and the chances of the FBI or the CIA coming to sort me out?

I was walking between two tall towers. New York had always seemed like Babel, but with the inhabitants too busy with repartee and recriminations to worry about getting up to heaven. They were perhaps jokers; but were there not less chancy ways of getting up to heaven?

I was standing on the edge of a pavement and there was a figure across the road that I thought I recognised. I waved. It was not Valerie; and perhaps this figure, along with other things from this time, exists only in my memory. A phrase had come into my mind – Towers fall by the force of gravity: God is the force of levity. I was pleased with this, and felt I should share it with someone – perhaps the person across the road? But in fact I remember very little of this moment, and nothing at all of what came just after; for as I stepped off the pavement (or did I not even do that?) a car or a van hit me and I became unconscious.

2

My first wife Valerie and I had met not long after the second world war. We each came from a privileged background. Valerie's was aristocratic; mine was a line of liberal academics. I used to joke – Call these privileges! They are more like the concrete in which gangsters used to encase victims' feet.

The 1950s are seen nowadays as a time of austerity, but to Valerie and me they offered liberation. For a few years after the war there was some observance of age-old conventions; but to challenge these now carried few penalties. Valerie and I first caught sight of each other across a crowded ballroom; grand dances had started up again to which anyone of privilege might be invited. Valerie and I eyed one another as if we each might be recognising a fellow agent in hostile territory. Later when I asked her to dance Valerie said 'I thought you looked like that murderer.' I said 'What, the one that cuts women up and dissolves them in the bath?' She said 'Yes.' It seemed we both thought we might marry.

This was some innocence – the belief that one can take on convention and make a nonsense of it. When we married we both intended to be faithful to each other; this was against the tradition of our families. But we felt it should be in our own tradition to explore. Valerie wanted to be a painter; I wanted to be a teacher whose ideas might alter the world.

For our honeymoon we went to Africa, because someone had given us airline tickets as a wedding present. Africa still seemed an unknown continent, with intimations of the heart of darkness. But here one might stumble on – new styles of liberation?

I do not know how to describe my marriage to Valerie without making the two of us seem somewhat freakish. But how should we seem, if we were to be part of a post-war world becoming different from the old?

When we married, Valerie and I were still technically virgins. This nowadays would seem freakish enough. But it seemed to us that to carry off being unconventional one needed to start from a state of innocence.

In Africa we stayed in a hotel at the edge of a hot sea. We walked hand in hand on the beach; we swam by moonlight. We had a way of going into the sea by which Valerie faced me and wrapped her arms and legs around me so that we became immersed in a position of making love.

We learned the intricacies of love-making by trial and error. Valerie endured a certain pain; but had been told that this was to be expected. And then how amazing that after such manoeuvrings something should happen so trans-cendentally out of one's control!

Then on the fourth day Valerie became ill. She had what at first we thought was food poisoning; then when the pain became bad she was rushed to the local hospital and was diagnosed as having acute appendicitis.

The doctor was a large African. He seemed to personify what could be life-giving at the heart of darkness. The wards of the local hospital were full; people lay two in a bed or sometimes on the floor. The doctor said 'This is an emergency: she must be operated on at once.' He himself was the surgeon. We were faced with not the choice but the necessity of handing over trust to what was like darkness. But had we not thought we would be ready for this? A space was cleared for a bed for Valerie in the corner of a storeroom. Valerie said 'I'm so sorry to be ruining your honeymoon.'

I said 'But it's you who will be having a miserable honeymoon!'

'You will be all right?'

'And you will too.'

She was operated on that evening. I stayed with her till she was wheeled into a space like a hotting-up furnace. Then I went to walk by the sea. The water looked oily as if it itself might catch fire. I did feel bereft. But I thought – Is there ever any virtue in pity or self-pity?

The doctor had said that he was having a birthday party in the hotel that night; he had invited me to join him, saying that it would take my mind off things. I had said 'You mean, if the operation has gone all right?' He had said 'Of course it will have gone all right!' I had thought – It will be interesting to see an African party.

I went to see Valerie in her small, cramped room. There was a nurse with her who said the operation had gone well; Valerie had now been sedated and would remain unconscious till morning. I thought – But of course I was anxious about the operation! I went back to the hotel and drank some whisky. Then I thought – Of course I should go to the party to show that I was not really anxious about the operation being done in a strange country.

The party was taking place out of doors, with tables and chairs beneath trees and a yellow moon. Those celebrating were mostly Africans; the white holiday-makers were keeping to the balconies or verandahs of their rooms or chalets. This was the time of the end of empire when old traditions were breaking up and there was uncertainty about what would be new commitments. I thought – But this is a time surely when an individual might affect the way things go.

The doctor was wearing a paper hat that had come from a cracker. A place had been kept for me at his table. The setting was theatrical-magical; with coloured lights hung from trees and black people dancing where a few years ago there would have been only whites. I sat and drank whisky. The music and dancing was in the style of what was known as 'high life' – a stately form of jiving or cake-walk in which couples followed one another round in an elegant procession. Across the table from me there was a woman who like me seemed to be on her own: she was neither black nor white but a striking bronze colour; in profile she was like the bust of Queen Nefertiti of Egypt. She appeared to be managing to keep her profile turned to all directions at once, as if this might be a means of discouraging people from talking to her. She watched the dancing. When a man came up to ask her to dance she smiled and shook her head, still without exactly turning to him. I had read that people who in those days were called 'coloured' often felt themselves at a disadvantage being stranded between black and white. I thought now – But surely they, and especially such a beautiful woman, should feel themselves representatives of a future to which everyone should aspire; in which all such preoccupation with colour will be smoothed and mingled out.

Also – Valerie and I are like coloureds! We will help to mingle things out.

I was thinking that sooner or later I should go up to the beautiful woman and ask her to dance. She would be likely to say no: but I would have paid my respects to the future. And because I was an outsider myself in this strange world, she might at least look at me. My action might be seen by others as improper, because the doctor would have told them of my wife languishing in hospital. But what should we – Valerie and I and now this Nefertiti-like woman – care about proprieties?

There came a time when everyone else seemed to be on the dance floor except the woman and I, so I went round the table feeling like a lonely gunfighter and I said 'Would you like to dance?'

When she did turn to me and was thus no longer in profile she was still like Queen Nefertiti but with something out of balance with the side of her face that had not hitherto been visible. It seemed somewhat immobile, tragic; as if she had suffered some loss. The eye that I had not seen before was sad; the eye that had been visible looked at me as if amused. She said 'I don't dance.'

'Why not?'

'Why do you want to know?'

'Because my wife is in hospital, and I'm feeling lonely, and people will be wondering what on earth I am doing asking you.'

'Yes I know.'

I thought – Know what – that my wife is in hospital? what people will be wondering? what I am doing asking you?

I was trying to think how to put this into communicable form when she said 'I've only got one leg.'

'Oh I see.'

'Do you?'

'I imagine so. How did you lose your leg?'

'I trod on a landmine when I was a child.'

'That's terrible. Did they give you a false leg?'

'I've got a peg. I didn't want something that looks like a false leg.'

'Yes I see that. Well if we danced, I could probably hold you just off the ground with your peg.'

She smiled with a smile that was strikingly affecting,

15

because it suddenly connected the two sides of her face. She said 'Would you like that?'

'Yes.'

'Come along then.' She stood up, balancing for a moment with her fingers on the table.

I said 'One might do the most magnificent *fouettés* on a peg.'

'Is that where you whirl round and round?'

'Yes.'

'I like that sort of dancing.'

I was thinking – I have both to take care not to look at her peg and also not to seem to be taking care not to look at her peg: this should not be too difficult. Her legs were in fact out of sight within a long skirt. She took my hand and led me to the dance floor. We danced sedately, at some distance from one another, and quite well.

She said 'How long have you been married?'

'This is the fourth day of our honeymoon.'

'Were you having a good time?'

'Yes.'

'What made you come to Africa?'

'Someone gave us air tickets as a wedding present.'

'Do you usually take advantage of what turns up?'

'Yes.'

We managed to do a few twirls with her moving under my arm. I thought – We are performing a courting ritual like birds. I was beginning to feel that it was my legs that were turning to water; that it was I who might topple on top of her, and she would prop me with the stability of her peg.

She said 'Do you want to know if the landmine did damage to me other than to my leg?'

I said 'Yes. I don't know. Did it?'

I thought – There's nothing wrong with your beautiful face!

She said 'I don't know.'

'But what did the doctors say?'

'Well in such circumstances they usually say what you want to hear.'

'Which was what?'

'I told them I didn't see how they could know.'

'And did they agree?'

'Sort of.'

'But then how would you know—'

'Exactly.'

'I see.'

'Do you?'

The music had stopped. It was as if we were in one of those situations in which two people who have been dancing do not want to let go. I had the imagination of a landmine going off between our legs.

I said 'I think so.'

She said again 'Come along then.'

She pulled away from me, still holding me by the hand, and led me off the dance floor. I thought – This seems to be happening without intention or volition. It was only a short distance to the beach, but we were not heading towards the beach. She said 'Is it hard for you, your wife being in hospital?'

'I suppose so.'

'Why just suppose?'

'She was worried I might be miserable.'

'And are you?'

'No.'

'So she might be pleased for you.'

'Yes. She's a good person.'

'Are you being good to me?'

'I hope so.'

'You don't have to.'

'No.'

'Which is your chalet?'

We were moving between the huts that were the main sleeping accommodation of the hotel. I was thinking – Well this may look like sleepwalking; but from the inside it is as if one had one's wits out like antennae.

We reached the chalet where Valerie and I had lived for three nights and three days. There were things of Valerie's scattered on the bed and on the floor. The woman like Nefertiti waited in the doorway while I turned on the light. She said 'Will you tell your wife about this?'

I said 'I don't know.'

'You keep saying you don't know.'

'Yes.'

'You don't know if you'd like to make love to me?'

'Well of course I'd like to.'

'I want to see if I can.'

'Yes I understand that.'

'But only if you want to.'

She went and sat on the edge of the bed. Her peg-leg stuck out like a small cannon. I said 'Yes I'd like to.'

She said 'When I lost my leg I was thirteen. I wanted to die. It was Dr Mboto who persuaded me not to.'

'He's the one who's operated on my wife?'

'Yes. Later I wanted him to make love to me, but he wouldn't.'

'Why not?'

'I suppose it was against his custom.'

'And it wouldn't be against mine?'

'I don't know. Now I'm saying I don't know.'

'Yes. Let me see your leg.'

She stood up, balancing on her good leg. She took off her skirt. Her peg-leg widened into a metal cup towards the top. There was a joint worked by a catch where there would have been her knee. Her thigh was a stump against which the metal cup was held by straps. These went between her legs and round her waist. I thought – This could be kinky?

I said 'Does it hurt?'

'Not all the time.'

'Will you take the peg off?'

'If you like.'

In my mind I was beginning a conversation with Valerie. I was saying – Well, what else could I do? Her leg was blown off by a mine when she was a child. Valerie was saying – Well what did you do? I was saying – She might have wanted me just to have a look.

The woman had taken off her peg and lain it on the bed. Then she sat on the edge again. The skin of her stump was wrinkled like old fruit. There were marks of scars, or discoloration, on her stomach and the inside of her thighs. She wore no undergarment. I thought – Her behind might not be marked. Then – No this is not kinky.

I said 'Can you make love to yourself? Have you tried?'

'Yes.'

'And it works?'

'I don't know exactly what's supposed to happen.'

'You want to know if it works inside?'

'Yes.'

'Some women say that doesn't happen anyway.' I smiled.

I had taken off some of my clothes. I thought – Well thank goodness I've had time to learn some of the tricks of the trade with Valerie!

I looked between her legs. It struck me that when one got as close as this, one person probably did not look all that different from another.

I said 'Is that hurting?'

'Not really.'

'It sometimes does anyway.'

19

'Yes that's all right.'

I leaned over her. I said 'You're very beautiful.'

'This really is extraordinarily good of you.'

'Not at all, it is a pleasure.'

'You won't tell your wife?'

'Will you tell Dr Mboto?'

'Dr Mboto says your wife is very beautiful.'

'Yes.'

'Oh God, what are you doing!'

'It's all right.'

'Oh God, oh God, it's so wonderful!'

'Yes.'

'I didn't know anything could be like this!'

I imagined myself saying to Valerie — She just wanted to find out, you see, if she could make love.

3

My first experience when I regained consciousness after having been hit by a car, a van, a juggernaut, or whatever, in New York, was of ambulance men trying to get me unstuck from – a bumper, a wall, a pavement? It was as if I were one of those wasps that has been swatted but goes on lethargically moving with bits of its inside hanging out. I realised later that I had been given morphine and that was why I was able to think my situation funny – how do you get flies off fly-paper without getting your fingers stuck, ha ha! I also learned that whoever was driving the vehicle that had hit me had jumped out and run away; after which I had apparently said to whoever had questioned me – Yes it's quite possible that someone was after me – the CIA, FBI, Mossad, KGB: one of those people who put poison on the spikes of their umbrellas. There is indeed something life-saving about morphine if you can think this sort of thing funny.

While I was not quite conscious I had felt I was having a conversation with Valerie in the hospital by the hot sea. She was saying – You say she just wanted you to have a look at her? I was saying – Well she had been blown up by a landmine when— Yes, yes, you've told me that. I had thought that I must say something to Valerie because the doctor had apparently told her that I was in good spirits on the dance floor, and so he must have seen me going off hand in hand with— I did not even know her name. But then I began to hurt violently, becoming conscious of being on the pavement again. Someone was trying to move or lift me. I yelled. A voice said 'We're only trying to free your leg!' I joked – 'Then try to free it along with the rest of me!' Once I had been given another shot of morphine I thought this witty. Englishmen are supposed to keep a stiff upper lip, or something or other, are they not? Had I not performed quite creditably? Was it because of my present predicament that I was remembering so vividly my encounter with the woman with the metal leg? And she had said – Oh thank you, thank you! I had said to Valerie – I think I did help her. Valerie had said – I'm sure you did. Then – But why are you telling me this now? I had said – Well we wanted no secrets between us, didn't we? Valerie had not answered. Valentina would have said – Oh fuck off!

Someone on the pavement was saying – By rights he should be dead. And I was wondering – What do you mean by rights? And the voice was saying – An artery was exposed, he should have got an infection. But then I became unconscious again, and heard no more of what I might have been learning.

The next time I became aware of my situation was when I was in what seemed to be the ante-room to an operating theatre. There was a man in a dark suit standing by me. He was saying 'Can you hear me?' I said in an RAF voice 'Loud and clear!' I suppose I was on morphine again. The man said 'You were saying something about what happened to you not being an accident, but that people were after you.'

'I said that out loud?'

'Apparently.'

22

'Well the CIA, Mossad, Al-Qaeda. I've been insulting them on television.'

'Can you remember who and how exactly?'

'The Mounties. The Rockies. They always get their man.'

'All right. The police will be along to take a statement later. In the meantime I'd like to get details of your insurance.'

'I don't think I have insurance. My wife usually does the insurance. The Bible seems to be against it.'

'How can we get in touch with your wife?'

'I don't want to worry her. She's lecturing in Scandinavia.'

'All right, I'll be back. It seems your pocketbook was taken when you were on the ground.'

'My pocketbook?'

'Your wallet.'

'Oh yes. Language is my speciality.'

'This is Sister Lisa, who will be with you when you come out of the theatre.'

'And then perhaps we can go on to a nightclub.'

'Sorry?'

'Nothing.' A tune had come into my head – Sister Lisa, Mona Lisa, I adore you!

I don't know for how long, for days or a week or two even, I was kept for the most part on morphine. My thigh-bone was splintered and could not immediately be set, so a temporary operation had been done, and then in bed my leg was suspended and stretched on a device like a hoist for getting cattle onto a ship. If I stayed still it only ached; but if I moved incautiously the ends of bones scraped against nerves and it was as if full torture treatment was under way and I wanted to shout – I'll tell you anything! But how could anyone think they might learn what was true?

I asked Sister Mona Lisa 'What is the significance of an artery being exposed?' She said 'You get an infection.' I said 'And that should kill you?'

'It can do.'

'And what would stop that?'

'They say it's as if just previously you'd had a shot of antibiotics.'

And I remembered—

But I thought I'd better keep quiet about what I remembered.

So in bed I tried to remain motionless in whatever knife-edge position I had managed to adopt, until Sister Lisa, the blessed Mona, came to give me my four-hourly shot of morphine. Then for two or three hours it did not much matter what was truth and what was not.

What I had remembered was that just before I had set out for New York I had had bad toothache from an abscess and my dentist had given me antibiotic pills to be taken at regular intervals, and so I had been taking these—

But people do not like to be told of good coincidences like this.

I had found I did not want to let Valentina know what had happened because she had arranged to go to a conference of psychotherapists in Sweden specifically to coincide with the time I was to be in New York, and I did not want my misfortune to harm the success that she was making of her life. Also I imagined her describing to her colleagues how I had got myself run over in New York because unconsciously I resented her not being with me; and this seemed funny but not all that funny. And had I not wanted to spend time on my own in New York? In order to – what? I could hardly pretend not to remember.

When I was pressed for information about my next of kin, Sister Lisa became intrigued. 'Have you really not got a wife or a partner?'

'All my identification was stolen while I was lying unconscious.'

'But that doesn't mean—'

'Why not? I was hoping to be free!'

'You're ghoulish!'

'Is that a word now – ghoulish?'

'It means mythical. Don't you watch that programme?'

'I watch almost everything else.'

A policeman did come to interview me briefly; and perhaps fortunately this happened when I was in pain, so I was not making jokes. He told me that the van that had run into me had been stolen, and this might be a new form of mugging which involved running into people and then going through their pockets as if to help them when they were on the ground. He held out little hope of my getting my wallet back. I thought – So here I am alone, penniless, without insurance, almost without identity: is not this the condition that I once thought necessary for enlightenment?

In fact I had told the hospital people my name and that of my hotel; and the television people had made solicitous inquiries.

Then the day came when the doctors were ready to set my leg and I was wheeled back to the theatre. I thought – To be truly enlightened should one not have a near-death experience?

This time when I emerged into consciousness Sister Mona Lisa was waiting for me and now with indeed a somewhat self-satisfied smile. She said 'Your wife has called and is coming to see you.'

'My wife has called and is coming to see me?'

'Yes. She said she saw it in the papers.'

'It was in the papers in Sweden?'

'She said she was in New York.'

'Good heavens!'

'I suppose you're going to say you haven't got a wife.'

'I'm most touched to find I have.'

'Well we must get you looking nice for her, mustn't we.'

But then – after I had been settled into a private room that had been newly allotted to me, and had dozed again and woken, and had had my hair brushed by Sister Lisa, and had then dozed again and woken – I wondered whether this time I had indeed been transported to some alternative existence because the person sitting by my bed was not Valentina but Valerie. At least she seemed to be Valerie. She was a bit older, with white hair. I said again 'Good heavens!'

She said 'I do hope you don't mind!'

I said 'As a matter of fact I was hoping to bump into you.'

'Quite a bump!'

'Yes.'

'How are you feeling?'

'It's good to see you. How did you get here?'

'I flew from California.'

'But I mean—'

'There was a piece in the papers. I rang the hospital. They said you hadn't got insurance. That's all they seem to care about. So I said I'd do the insurance.'

'You'd do the insurance? Pay the bills?'

'Otherwise they throw you out into the street. I've always wondered if that's true.'

'That's extraordinarily good of you!'

'Or rather Charlie will pay the bills. He's very rich.'

'Charlie von Richtoven? You're still with Charlie?'

'He isn't really "von".'

'Adam says he's made his billions from drugs.'

'But druggie drugs or drugstore drugs—'

'Oh I see.'

'Though I think he thinks what's the difference.'

I had the impression that what was happening made absolute sense, though I would not have been able to say just what this was.

Valerie said 'I think the people at the hospital got the impression I was your wife.'

'Well that could make sense.'

'I thought it would save hassle.'

'Yes indeed.'

'All that stuff about being married in a church. Although I remember we didn't think much about that at the time.'

Valerie had always had fair hair, and the skin of her face had seemed almost translucent. It now had faint wrinkles on it as if recognition were now required of its fragility.

A woman came in holding a credit card and a payment slip; she handed these to Valerie, and Valerie signed. I thought – She has not remarried? Her name is still the same?

The woman said 'So that's taken care of.' She went out.

I said 'I was thinking about us just before I was hit by a bus.'

'I thought it was a removals van.'

'You remember that time when we were on our honeymoon—'

'Yes I remember our honeymoon—'

'And I bumped into that woman with the wooden leg—'

'You said it was metal.'

'Yes. And you thought I must have been to bed with her—'

'Well of course you had been to bed with her!'

'Did you mind?'

'Of course I minded!'

'I'm so sorry.'

'Oh well, what does it matter.'

'I wanted to ask you – Do you think I shouldn't have told you?'

'Of course you should have told me! I mean no of course you shouldn't have told me. But anyway you didn't. Dr Mboto did. He said you were very good to her. The brute.'

'He was jealous.'

'About her?'

'Or about you.'

'Oh yes, of course I went to bed with Dr Mboto! The bed was just there! What else could I do? I think she was very clever.'

'Clever?'

'Oh all right, not clever.'

I was feeling both exhilarated and exhausted. I could feel pain breaking through the morphine. I said 'Dearest Valerie, it's such a wonder seeing you!'

She said 'Et in arcadia ego. I've never known what that means.'

'It means – We'll always have the amusement arcade—'

'Which we didn't have before?'

'Oh but we did!'

'Yes we did. But I mustn't tire you. I'll come back tomorrow.'

'Yes do.'

'Oh yes, there's something I wanted to tell you about Adam.'

'Adam?'

'Our son Adam. You know, Adam! He wants to adopt a baby.'

'He's got his girlfriend pregnant? Who is his girlfriend?'

'No he says it's not that.'

'What is it then?'

'He just wants to adopt a baby.'

With the morphine wearing off I was beginning to see Valerie more dispassionately. We were both old and frail but had succeeded in keeping our heads below the clouds and above the pit. I thought – How can it ever have made sense to quarrel?

Sister Mona Lisa put her head round the door. She looked

as usual enigmatic. I said 'Is it time for my morphine?' Valerie said 'It's all right, I'm just going.'

Sister Lisa said 'There's some query about the credit card.'

Valerie said 'Oh dear, perhaps I've overspent again. But it'll be all right. Charlie tops it up.'

I said to Sister Lisa 'Tell them he's the head of Von Richtoven Chemicals.'

Sister Lisa said 'Who?' Then to Valerie 'I think you'd better tell them that.'

Valerie stood up. At the door she said 'I think Adam's got some idea about how it's no good going on about how one's parents didn't bring one up right if one doesn't have a go oneself. And I tell him that if he can think that, then his parents must have brought him up right.'

I said 'Yes that makes sense.'

4

When I had been given my next shot of morphine I began to feel that all the problems of the world might be solvable – in the style, that is, that was being so valiantly demonstrated by Valerie and me. It had once seemed that envy and resentment must be advantageous weapons in the evolutionary battle for survival; but were not Valerie and I showing that if one kept one's head in what were naturally difficult situations, then in spite of temptations to indulge in rage or self-pity, with luck and endurance things might turn out all right?

This was innocence? Decadence? Sophistication? Or simply the effects of morphine.

Not long after our return from our honeymoon Valerie announced that she wished to go for a term at least to an art school in Paris. She had wanted to do this for some time, but had been prevented by the conventions of her upper-class family, which paid lip-service to art so long as one of them did not want to be an artist. It had been one of our hopes in marrying that we might break away from such a tradition. Valerie wanted to go to Paris because this was where she understood that the best painting was still being done. I had by this time been offered a junior lectureship in London, which it seemed sensible for me at the time to take up, even if I broke away from an academic career later.

I said to Valerie 'But of course you must go to Paris! You'll feel resentment if you don't. And we can write each other marvellous letters saying how absence makes our hearts grow fonder, which will one day make us immortal.'

'But you will miss me?'

'Of course I'll miss you!'

'Very much?'

'Yes very much.'

'Then all right I'll go.'

While Valerie had been convalescing from her operation she had spent a lot of time in bed both before and after we got back from Africa. I would sit with her in the evenings and read to her from the books I had collected in order to brush up on my knowledge of European literature. I read aloud the whole of Milton's *Paradise Lost*; I embarked on Dante's *The Divine Comedy*, but halfway through the 'Inferno' Valerie said it was making her feel ill and asked me to stop. We tried Homer's *Iliad* but both got exhausted by the repetitions of people bashing one another. Valerie said 'If these are the backbone of European literature, no wonder we're in such a state of collapse.'

I said 'It's what life's like. Literature is supposed to say what life's like.'

'Why not try to make it better?'

'Because people would then feel they were being got at, which they don't like. And anyway, efforts to change things usually make them worse.'

'But can't people see how all this is describing a terrible way to live? I'd rather be dead.'

'That's what the Greeks used to say.'

'What?'

'If there's one thing better than being dead, it's not to have been born.'

'But Dante could still get himself off by imagining people boiling in hell.'

'Well Milton's OK.'

'I don't think Milton's OK. Milton's God is a role model for every European power freak and bully.'

I was remembering this as I lay in my hospital bed in New York. Valerie came to see me on three consecutive days. I thought – Well she has become my good angel!

She did not tell me much more about our son Adam wanting to adopt a baby: she said she could not make out what he was up to herself. I wondered – He wants to start some post-Miltonic dynasty? Some environment that might weave both heaven and hell into a pattern? Adam was at the moment in South America working for Valerie's friend Charlie Richtoven, who was said to be trying to corner, or regulate, or prevent, the traffic in illicit drugs. (These activities might not be seen as different?) Valerie said Adam would come and see me on his way to a new job in Afghanistan. (This was where my blessed morphine came from?) But at the moment I was happy looking not forward but back to the best of times Valerie and I had had together before she started going to Paris.

I had tried to explain about Milton. I had said 'But God had to look like a shit if humans were to be free.'

'Why?'

'Because humans had to learn things for themselves. They had to stop thinking that God was so wonderful running everything. He wanted us to be free. He just guaranteed us our freedom.'

'But humans don't learn.'

'We've only had a few tens of thousands of years!'

'I don't think we'll ever learn.'

'Well I suppose God has to keep on hoping.'

I remembered Valerie's distrustful look. I thought – Well she might learn.

She said 'And this is the sort of stuff you're going to teach?'

'And what we might be learning but haven't yet.'

'I think we'd be better packed up and started again.'

'But that would be sad.'

'Why?'

'Well there are good times after all.'

Now, on the third day of Valerie visiting me in hospital in New York, we were settling into a routine that we looked forward to, and she was saying 'I read what you write. And you're not still teaching that old stuff.'

'What stuff?'

'About things having to be packed up.'

'That wasn't me, that was you!'

'But something changed you.'

'Oh well, you know some of it.'

'When you went to Iran?'

'Yes, things turn up. What's called chance.'

'You mean God does stick his oar in?'

'Oh yes, that's called chance. But there's still something keeping the thing afloat.'

'So that's what you learn?'

Sister Lisa put her head round the door. She needed to do this less frequently now that I was coming off morphine. But she could still appear conspiratorial. She said 'You've got a telephone call from Sweden.'

I said 'Oh dear.'

'It's from someone who says she's on her way to see you.'

'How long does it take to get here from Sweden?'

Valerie said 'Must take a day.'

Sister Lisa said 'I told her the doctor was with you so you couldn't speak to her at the moment.'

I said 'Quite right.'

Valerie said 'I must be going.'

I said to Sister Lisa 'Is there anything else she said? Did she say she was my wife?'

Sister Lisa said 'Yes she did as a matter of fact.' She came on into the room. I thought – How terrifying if the Mona Lisa got down from her enigmatic rock!

I said 'I'll explain.'

Valerie said 'I'd like to hear that!' She went to the door. Then 'But don't you say there are things you can't explain?'

I thought – What miraculous timing that I've been able to see Valerie for these three days!

Sister Lisa said 'What shall I say if she rings back?'

Valerie said 'Tell her the doctor's gone.' And then to me 'Give my love to old Concertina.' Then 'No, Valentina, Valentina!' She frowned and tapped her wrist, as if to admonish herself.

I said 'It's been wonderful seeing you. Keep in touch.'

Valerie said 'Yes I will.' She went out.

Sister Lisa moved round the room tidying things ostentatiously. She said 'You don't have to explain anything.'

I said 'But I do! This is extraordinarily important! It does actually make complete sense! The one who's been coming here is my first wife, Valerie: we're divorced, but there were one or two things to be sorted out. The one who's on her way is my second wife, to whom I'm married now.'

'So you're not a Mormon.'

'No.'

'I once knew a Mormon. The wives seemed to like it.'

'Valerie's family's Catholic.'

'I see. And what are you?'

'I'm a believer in keeping your wits about you, and getting

down from your high horse and giving it a slap so that it disappears into the bush where with luck things sort themselves out.'

Sister Lisa said 'And what's this second wife called?'

'Valentina.'

'Valerie and Valentina. Did you plan that?'

'No.'

'But Valerie's the one who's paying for you.'

'Yes. She's rich. I mean her boyfriend's very rich.'

'Her boyfriend? And what does he make of this?'

'I don't know.'

'And this is what you call things sorting themselves out?'

'Yes.'

'So what are you going to tell Valentina—'

'Ah. I don't know.'

'She's not a Mormon or a Catholic?'

'No, she's a psychotherapist.'

'And what do they believe?'

'That you can learn to live with some things if you work to sort them out.'

'That sounds more sensible.'

'Yes it does. We'll have to see.'

'This is better than TV.'

Valentina telephoned again when she was changing planes at Heathrow. She said 'Why didn't you tell me you'd been knocked down by a bus?'

'It wasn't a bus, it was a mysterious assailant.'

'So you're not really hurt.'

'Of course I'm really hurt! I've been in agony! I may never walk again! But I didn't want to muck up your conference.'

'Try again.'

'I couldn't bear the thought of you all going on about how much I must be missing you to have got myself knocked down by a bus.'

'The nurse I spoke to was most peculiar. She sounded as if she were in love with you.'

'No, I'm a bit in love with her. She's called Sister Mona Lisa. Do you remember that film about a black tart?'

'No.'

'Well it'll be wonderful to see you.'

'I'll be with you in about eight hours.'

I tried to doze off, but now that I was not being allowed so much morphine my ribs as well as my leg were hurting. I asked Sister Lisa for another shot. She said 'You can have one in six hours, before Valentina arrives.'

I tried to go back to thinking of the early years of Valerie's and my marriage. What had gone wrong? Or had nothing gone wrong – everything had happened for the best in the best of all possible worlds.

Valerie took to going regularly for a few weeks a year to her art school in Paris. At the end of one of these sessions she turned up with a young Frenchman whom she said she had met on the boat: he was a student on his way to do postgraduate work in London. Valerie said he was a nuclear physicist and had nowhere to stay. I said 'So if we don't offer him suitable accommodation he might blow us all up.'

Valerie said 'I thought you might like talking to him.'

I thought – Well I might, mightn't I?

Valerie said 'It's you who've taught me to take advantage of things that turn up!'

So Valerie's Frenchman came to stay and he was small and sombre and good-looking, and he and Valerie had long talks in the evenings, facing each other in the small window-seat, about – what – fusion versus fission? the danger of a rogue neutron? This was at the height of the Cold War and there were threats and counter-threats, the deployment of lies and deception becoming as important as that of bombs. I had thought – Well at least if Valerie and the Frenchman are in the house I'll be able to keep an eye on them. Yet I did not want to appear to need to keep an eye on them. How might this be resolved – by some trick?

I discovered that the Frenchman fancied himself at ping-pong. I dug out my childhood table and set it up in the cramped space in the entrance hall of our lodgings. The Frenchman and I began to play in the evenings and some-times he would beat me twenty-one—nineteen and sometimes I would beat him twenty-one—ninteteen, and so we had to have just one more game, and so on. And Valerie would sit on the window-seat sewing.

After a time I said to her 'How long is he staying?'

'Just until his college finds him a room.'

'I'm being driven demented!'

'You're not. You're loving it.'

'I didn't know he'd be so good at ping-pong!'

'I'm not talking about ping-pong.'

'Oh I see.'

So after not too long the Frenchman left. And I thought – She cannot have been all that attracted to him.

I was remembering this while I was in the hospital in New York hanging on for my rare shot of morphine before Valentina's arrival.

When Valentina came in she looked round my spacious private room, and after she had given me a kiss she said 'How on earth were you given this?'

'All right I'll come clean! You won't believe it!'

'No I don't suppose I will.'

'Well, Valerie happened to be in New York, and she read about me in the papers, and she rang the hospital to ask how I was, and they told her I hadn't got insurance—'

'But you have got insurance! I always get you insurance!'

'But my wallet was stolen as I was lying in the street. They call it a pocketbook.'

37

'I know they call it a pocketbook!'

'Anyway, Valerie offered to cover my expenses.'

'The bitch!'

'Otherwise I'd have been thrown out on the street.'

'Of course you wouldn't have been thrown out on the street!'

'And she hasn't married again, so we still have the same name, and so without too much fuss they accepted her credit card.'

Valentina seemed to think about this. She said 'What's happened to that man with the obviously bogus name?'

'I think he's around somewhere.'

'What does Valerie look like nowadays? Still like death slightly *chambré*?'

'I've been in great pain! I may never walk again!'

'So you keep saying. Well I'm sorry.'

'Would you have liked me to have rung you up and moaned and said how could you have let me come on my own to New York?'

'I've said I'm sorry!'

'Oh that's all right. Have you been having a good time?'

'I haven't had any sleep for two nights!'

'Well I think it's angelic of you to have got here.'

'I've had a word with the doctor. Of course you'll walk again!'

Valentina unloaded from a bag some chocolate, some fruit juice and some grapes. I said 'Thank you.'

She said 'And if I go back to the hotel now, for some sleep, Valerie won't suddenly pop out of the woodwork?'

'No, she's just in the bathroom having a pee.'

'Well I'm glad you're so cheery.'

'I'm not, I'm in extreme anxiety, but that is supposed to keep you on your toes, if I still have any toes, and it's so good seeing you.'

38

Soon after Valentina had gone Valerie telephoned. I imagined Sister Lisa at a switchboard masterminding the timings. Valerie said 'I just wanted to check that everything is all right.'

'Yes, it's fine.'

'You can blame everything on me you know.'

'No it's all right.'

'Oh dear, then that's good, isn't it?'

'Look, before you go, I just want to ask you something.'

'What?'

'Did you get up to anything with that Frenchman?'

'Which Frenchman?'

'The one who came to stay. The one who played ping-pong.'

'Oh that one!'

I thought – Damn, I shouldn't have asked!

She said 'No of course I didn't!' Then 'But I'm glad you asked.'

'Why?'

'Work it out. You taught me to be clever.'

I thought – Because it shows I was jealous?

After a time Sister Lisa came in to what she called 'settle me down' and I said 'I need to be settled! This is all getting too much for me!'

Sister Lisa said 'It's not, you're loving it!'

'Yes. I'm so transparent. That's what everyone tells me.'

'You should have married someone straightforward like me.'

'I don't know. I don't think life is straightforward.'

'You're always saying you don't know!'

'Yes. Someone else once said that to me.'

'Who?'

'I don't know. I didn't know her name.'

5

Valerie's and my marriage showed signs of strain when our son Adam was on his way to being born. Valerie felt that she could not now live as she wanted as a painter: she resented not the baby but the feeling of impossibility – it was so corny! I could keep out of the way of such dilemmas; but was not such fatherly evasion corny?

By this time I was a junior fellow at an Oxford college and was gathering ideas for my first book. I did not fit easily into the social life of the college; few dons as young as I were married, and I suppose Valerie and I were seen as aloof. Valerie had fixed up a studio in a spare room at the back of our flat; she no longer travelled to Paris, but she held to the idea that painters should be dedicated to their work. When she tried not to let pregnancy distract her this suited me because I had a room in college where, when I was not seeing pupils, I could get on with research for my book. I could justify staying clear of Valerie because it seemed that this was what she wanted.

My book was to be an inquiry into the nature of language – both its origins and the styles in which it was used. A traditional theory suggested that human language had evolved, and had never quite broken away, from the bonding and warning cries of birds and animals – used as an aid to hunting and for protection against predators. And indeed in the West public language seemed to be used less for the passing of accurate information than as a means of attack, defence, complaint, self-justification. Reason could be used to give backing to these.

There was a gloss on this theory that was coming into fashion. This suggested that private rather than public discourse had its origin in the way in which apes, our evolutionary neighbours, spend so much time grooming themselves and one another looking for lice and fleas. This was a ritual for social bonding not dependent on hunting or danger. Such an idea appealed to me because it seemed so relevant to the backbiting and indeed nit-picking character-istics of the academic society in which I lived.

I also wanted to ask – What might be imagined as the pre-Babel language by means of which in the biblical story humans had been building their tower up to heaven? Of course this was a myth. But myths give intimations of what people have instincts about and can give expression to in no better way.

But also I wanted to say – Surely what distinguishes humans most unequivocally from animals is their faculty for self-criticism and humour: also possibly some form of self-creation.

When Valerie became pregnant I used to tell myself that I should hurry home in the evenings in order to keep her company. But I could also tell myself that she was trying to get some work done before the baby arrived and so my presence would be oppressive. So would not a proper compromise be if I stopped off on the way home at the local pub? And would not this be made even more correct if I thought such a rationalisation funny?

I might have asked Valerie what she would prefer; but this would only have been putting an added burden of decision onto her. And so on.

I had a friend called Tom who was a junior fellow at a neighbouring college. Tom had as gloomy a view as I did of academic life and practice, and he extended this to the general state of the world. He would hold forth – Humans have been wired up wrongly: they've been programmed to believe in contradictory premises: Love your neighbour but make a million before you're thirty: turn the other cheek but never apologise, never explain. So they fuse: crash.

I would say – But they're given the chance to see this as funny.

Tom was the first person I knew who seemed seriously to believe that humans should be eliminated and some other species thus be given the space to evolve in their place. He would say – Humanity is manure. It should be dug in.

I would say – But manure has the function of encouraging growth.

– It's people that are manure; it's their ideas, inventions, artworks, that are flowers.

– But something might change within oneself as a result of ideas, inventions?

I got in the habit of meeting Tom in the pub on my way home in the evenings. I do not know why I enjoyed his company at this time except that I felt dissatisfied with my own pessimism and needed his to challenge mine. So we would brood or guffaw like other men above our pints of beer.

Tom would complain about women. He had got into a rut of finding what he thought was his ideal woman, then after a few days his hopes being dashed by grave flaws in her personality. I would say 'All right, this is how you've been programmed. So have a look at the wiring.'

Tom would say 'It's all right for you, you've got money.'

'I haven't, Valerie's family have got money. And what's that got to do with it?'

'You're cushioned. Protected.'

'Yes.'

'So what's your problem.'

'I haven't got a problem. Valerie's pregnant.'

'So you've told me. Presumably she wanted it.'

'I think it just happened.'

'Women aren't illogical.'

'Neither are men. They get hooked on women.'

I wondered – Are Tom and I like apes looking for fleas? When Valerie and I talked I tried to explain – 'Academics usually talk in abstractions: Tom and I at least talk of flesh and blood.'

'I thought you said you grumbled about women.'

'He grumbles. I try to inoculate him.'

'Against what. Against me?'

Tom's great love was Shakespeare, about whom he lectured and wrote articles. He saw Shakespeare's famous women as ineluctable and lethal – Lady Macbeth, Cleopatra. And he saw victims such as Ophelia or Desdemona as goats tethered in a clearing to lure tigers to their doom.

I said 'But it's men who are the killers.'

Tom said 'Women are killers without even knowing it.'

'But if men know it, they should be able to stop. And they don't. They're like babies.'

'Then why aren't women better at looking after babies?'

'Perhaps men should be looking after babies and women should be running the world.'

'But they don't want to, they want to go on complaining about men.'

'And what do you think you do?'

'Stick my neck out.'

43

'Yes, like Ophelia, Desdemona—'

And so on. I thought – We are not even like apes, we are like undergraduates.

Once during these days I took Tom home to meet Valerie. Valerie looked exhausted. Tom circled round her as if she were a princess locked up in a tower and he was considering himself as her executioner. She asked Tom what he did apart from his teaching and he said – as if this should impress her – that he wrote articles for the *London Review of Books* and the *Times Literary Supplement*. Valerie said 'That must be a terrible job!' Tom looked away as if she had delivered her own death sentence. I thought – What she said was ridiculous: but she is guarding herself and her young from predators.

After Tom had gone she said 'I'm sorry, but I thought him a dreadful man.'

'I know he's annoying, but he's not politically correct, so he's useful for me to try out ideas on. And I wanted to show you that he really existed – this man I meet in the pub.'

'But he doesn't really exist. He only sniffs around you because he thinks you're glamorous.'

'But I'm not.'

'I know that, but he doesn't.'

'I think he thinks you're glamorous. He's scared of you.'

And so on. I thought – This is the sort of conversation people have when things are going wrong with a marriage.

Then when the time came for Adam to be born there was found to be something wrong with Valerie's blood – its sugar content or whatever. So I went with her to the hospital to have tests, and while we were waiting for the results I had to leave her, because that evening I was giving a lecture. And after it I found a message for me at the college saying would I go to the hospital as soon as possible; and when I got there I found that Valerie had been sedated and there had been talk about whether the baby would have to be induced. I told the

44

doctor I was sure that Valerie would want the birth to be as natural as possible, but of course he must do what he thought necessary. He said that anyway they would do nothing till the morning, and in the meantime Valerie would be sleeping, so he advised me to go home and myself to get some sleep. The hospital promised to telephone me if anything in the situation changed.

So I walked home thinking about the time when Valerie had become ill on our honeymoon, and I had what I called bumped into the woman who looked like Nefertiti.

Then when I got to our apartment building I found Tom peering in through a ground-floor window. He said 'Where have you been? I've been looking for you for hours!'

I said 'Valerie's had to go to the hospital. They're keeping her there.'

'I've had the most terrible time! I must talk to you.'

'The baby may have to be induced.'

'But it's not an emergency?'

'I don't know.'

I remembered – It was the woman like Nefertiti who told me I was always saying I don't know.

Tom said 'Two days ago I met the perfect woman, the one whom I know I could spend the rest of my life with. And now she's walked out.'

'But why?'

'I think this is the end of the road for me.'

'Come in and have a drink.'

I was thinking – This should be the end of the road for my relationship with Tom, so let's drive it over the cliff.

But then – Do you think there might be some connection between my being nice to Tom in these circumstances and no harm coming to Valerie and the baby?

This was the sort of thing that had come into my head when I was with the woman like Nefertiti.

Tom said 'And please don't think this is funny.'

'No I don't think it's funny.'

'It's all the fault of her guru, Rum Baba. He's told her that any other commitment gets in the way of enlightenment.'

I said 'Is he really called Rum Baba?'

'I knew you wouldn't be serious!'

'But why are you telling me this now?'

'I've got no one else to turn to!'

I was worrying – Why hadn't Valerie left a message for me?

Tom followed me into the sitting room and I poured us both a drink. I said 'But this is the sort of thing you've always expected of women.'

'Does that make it any better?'

'It might do. If you see that.'

'It's all right for you, you can stand it.'

'Stand what?'

'The racket. I don't know how you do it.'

'But I don't do it! I'm tired and worried! I want to get some sleep.'

'We always meet in the pub after your lectures.'

'God damn it, Tom, you're jealous. You want to fuck up me and Valerie and the baby!'

'That's a terrible thing to say!'

'Yes isn't it. But if you like you can sleep on the sofa.'

I went through into the bedroom and sat on the edge of the bed. I wondered – Might I rather by getting angry with Tom be defending Valerie and the baby?

– Are there not strange spirits at work at the birth of a baby?

When I did lie down I couldn't sleep. Imponderables whirled in my head – Should I have cancelled my lecture; should I have stayed all night at the hospital, should I never have let Tom's dislike of women into our house? Or might not Tom after all be like Mephistopheles who 'wills evil but engenders good'? (Which part of Faust did that come from?)

And was I then suffering from delusions of omnipotence like Faust, imagining myself to be able to influence things mysteriously as if I were present at the first nano-seconds of the universe when everything was still as one – good and evil, birth and death, orderliness and chaos. I wondered if at this moment Valerie's and my child might be being born.

At the beginning of the universe there was no language? There was said to have been just one – what was it – Word?

Eventually I must have slept because I was suddenly aware of a bright light coming in through the window. I panicked slightly and rang the hospital and asked for news of Valerie. After a long pause I was put through to a ward where a woman's voice said 'You have a beautiful baby boy!' I said 'But you promised to ring me!' The voice said 'You've got nothing to worry about, mother and child are doing fine.' I said 'But she'd have expected me to be there!' The voice said 'You can see them now just for a moment.' I thought – But it's all the fault of Tom! If he hadn't been here I'd have rung the hospital sooner! Then – But why didn't Valerie get the hospital to ring me? Had she somehow known I was with Tom, and had thus wanted to take this out on me? Did we all want to be martyrs?

Then – Oh all right, this is a test for me not to blame anyone except myself.

– Or perhaps not to blame anyone at all.

I was putting on some clothes. I was planning how to get rid of Tom and never speak to him again. I went through to the sitting room, but he was not there. I thought – Well at least that's a mercy! Then I ran all the way to the hospital telling myself – But none of this matters! Valerie and the baby are all right.

When I got to the hospital it was still early and I went up to the ward and Valerie was sitting up in bed with her golden hair down over her shoulders and looking composed and beautiful. She said 'Where have you been? They couldn't find you.' I said 'I came last night when you were sleeping, and they told me to go away until the morning and they promised to ring me if anything happened earlier.' She said 'But didn't they ring you?' I said 'When?' I was thinking – If Tom answered the telephone in the sitting room and didn't tell me I'll kill him. Then – But this is absurd, it would have rung in the bedroom. Valerie said 'Anyway, here you are now, and it's nice of you to have worried.' I said 'Did you have an awful time?' She said 'It wasn't too bad actually.' I leaned over to kiss her and she offered me her cheek as she usually did and I felt I might collapse on top of her, but I didn't. And then I thought – Perhaps in fact she told them not to ring me, because she wanted to say she'd done it all on her own. And why not? I said 'Where's the baby?' She said 'They've taken him away to do something to him.' I said 'But he's all right?' She said 'Yes he's fine.' I sat down beside her. I thought – And maybe this sort of trust is the point of a marriage.

6

When Adam came to see me in the hospital in New York he bounded into my room, huge and ungainly. He said 'No one believes I have a father as old as you, I mean no one believes you have a son as young as me.' He laughed. He leaned over to embrace me and it seemed he might topple over on top of me.

Sister Lisa had followed him in. I had told her Adam was my son by my first wife Valerie. She said in her best conspiratorial manner 'I'll tell you when anyone's coming.'

Adam said 'Like the chicken or the egg. Do you know that story?'

I said 'No.'

'Which came first. When they're in bed together.'

I thought about this. I said 'Oh I see.' I laughed. 'That's very clever.'

Sister Lisa said 'What's the answer?'

Adam said 'One says to the other – Now we'll be able to answer that question.'

Sister Lisa said to me 'Perhaps you'll be able to tell me later.'

When she had gone Adam said 'She's a bit in love with you.'

I said 'She thinks we're better than *EastEnders*.'

'And so we are.'

'Valerie says you think that parents bring their children up all wrong.'

'The parents in *EastEnders*.'

'Were we any better? Valerie seems to think that's why you want to adopt a baby.'

Adam sat down. It was as if he were considering this question for the first time. He said 'Ah. Yes.' Then 'People get hooked on their parents. Their parents both demand this and then resent it: that's the hook.'

'It's called love?'

'Ah. That's the question.'

'What started you on this?'

'You did. So you see you were a good parent!'

A conversation with Adam was always something of a steeplechase: you leapfrogged over conversational conventions. I thought – But in hospital I can have a rest between jumps.

I said 'I thought as parents we were pretty ridiculous.'

'Well you might have been what other people called ridiculous, but that could be an indication of being all right.'

'So you don't feel hooked—'

'No, I feel thrown back into the sea.'

'Having learnt something?'

'And able to go on learning.'

'Yes I see.'

The last time I had seen Adam he had said he was about to set off for South America to report on the war that was going on between American-backed forces and the farmers in the hills who were growing crops from which to make cocaine. He had for some time been a member of a humanitarian organisation that looked out for injustice and atrocities and publicised them when they occurred.

I said 'And you want to adopt a baby that won't find itself hooked?'

'Oh well, it's a bit more complicated, but that's a way of putting it.'

'A baby from where – Colombia? Afghanistan?'

'Or from anywhere. I rather like the idea of it having been thrown from a boat-load of asylum-seekers about to be arrested, and being washed up on the shore.'

'Yes I see.'

'I think everyone should be vaguely, I mean metaphorically, ready to rescue anyone, whether or not with a boat-hook.'

'But is that possible?'

'Well it's tricky.'

I tried to think about this. I thought I could see that Adam might not want to talk about it directly. I said 'You mean, it might be better if a girl didn't know its mother?'

Adam said 'Do you know that Irish joke? A girl goes to her mother and says – Ma, I'm pregnant. And her mother says – Are you sure it's yours?'

I said 'Yes that's funny.' Then 'But it could be yours?'

'Oh yes indeed.'

'And you don't want it to have a mother?'

'Or its mother doesn't want to be a mother.'

'I see.'

'Do you?'

'No.'

'But you see why you were a good parent!'

I was beginning to feel stretched, as I so often did with Adam, between the impression that I was learning something important, and that he was a conjuror aiming to put me in a box and saw me in two. But then at the end would I jump out miraculously all in one piece!

I said 'You think that if everyone can be encouraged to see

they're dependent on either no one or everyone, and so feel beholden to no one or everyone instead of being stuck with a family or a tribe or a religion, then they won't have the experience of their insides being pulled out by a hook.'

'And they won't want to go fishing.'

'They're all in the sea.'

'Yes. Unlike Oedipus. Electra. Who got landed.'

'Indeed.'

I was beginning to feel so attenuated that it might be better if I were sawn up for comfort.

I said 'Well, parents should feel a bit dependent on one another, surely, so that children can see what dependency is.'

'Oh yes, indeed.'

'I've been seeing a bit of Valerie recently.'

'Yes, so she said. Good.' Then 'Do you think that was why you had your accident?'

'Why?'

Adam put a hand up to his eyes. He seemed to grope with his other hand for a chair on which he might stretch out and put his feet up. He said 'I was going to ask you something particular as a matter of fact. But I now don't know if it's after all the point.'

I said 'What—'

'Valerie said that the people at the hospital took her to be still your wife. I had wondered if in fact that might make it easier for me to adopt the baby – I mean if the baby could be seen to be getting respectable grandparents.'

'I don't know, would it?'

'I don't suppose so. The idea came into my head. But now that seems to have happened anyway.'

'What—'

'I mean I wanted you and Valerie to be all right. But now in fact the whole plan, process, is moving on to something different. But I've always known that.'

'What—'

'I mean it's a step. Not an answer.'

I thought – No indeed. Do I know what he is talking about?

Sister Lisa put her head round the door. She said 'Someone's on their way up. I think it's Valentina.'

Adam said 'I'm going.' Then 'Do you hear anything of Cathy?'

'Cathy?'

'Your stepdaughter, Cathy.' He went to the door and peered out cautiously.

I said 'What about Cathy?' I had the impression that having been sawn in half, the time was coming where I would be expected to jump out of the box.

Adam said 'I'll come again. Like the chicken. Or the egg.' He went to the door. 'Or I'll see you in London.'

I said 'Yes, you do that.'

I was thinking – He mentioned Cathy on purpose, so that I might have the chance of working things out for myself.

He stood half out of the door with his back pressed against the frame as if theatrically trying to keep out of sight. He said with a foreign accent 'You can't make-a da omelette without breakin' da egg.' Then he went out.

Sister Lisa appeared and leaned against the door-frame as Adam had done. I thought – This is like a ballet.

Valentina came past her into the room. She said 'That was Adam.'

I said 'Yes. It's one of the roles he likes to play; that of a Swiss gynaecologist.'

'Why?'

'I don't know.'

I thought – If you don't know you're in the dark, you can't work things out.

53

Valentina put down parcels, bags, scarves, on the floor. She said 'What a day!'

I said 'What's been happening with Cathy?'

'Cathy?'

'Your daughter Cathy.'

'I know my daughter Cathy.'

'Is she still in Bethlehem?'

'Why?'

'Adam wants to adopt a baby.'

I was thinking – Cathy, being in the same sort of business as Adam, wouldn't want to have to make such decisions: she'd want to watch things working out in their own peculiar way.

Cathy was in a do-gooding set-up like Adam, except that her lot seemed stuck on the virtue of being martyrs. She had gone out to Israel as one of a group who said they intended to interpose themselves between warring Palestinian and Jewish factions, even if this meant—

Valentina said 'You're not making sense.'

I said 'No, I've been knocked on the head.'

'You're perfectly all right. Why does Adam want to adopt a baby?'

'Oh, you know that! Who told you?'

'You did.'

'Oh yes. I suppose he wants to start a new human race.'

'That's insane.'

'Yes. But it's a way of talking.'

Sister Lisa had gone out of the room holding her head. I was trying to think of too many things at once. Valentina said 'That woman acts as if she's in love with you.'

I said 'What happened to those people who were holed up in the Church of the Nativity?'

'That was ages ago. You watch too much television.'

'I haven't watched any television here.'

'Why not?'

'I've been trying to work things out about myself.'

'I can't think which would be more depressing.'

'Oh all right!'

I tried to remember my last contacts with Cathy. I had not seen her for about a year. Hadn't she come back from Bethlehem? Had she gone out again? When she had been a child I had seemed to be a bit in love with Cathy. I said 'When are we going home?'

'As soon as maybe. The doctor says if we go first class you can get a seat with your leg sticking out.'

'Valerie will pay.'

'Valerie won't pay.'

'I once knew a woman who had a metal leg that stuck out like a cannon.'

'So you've told me.'

'I have?'

'Often.'

'Oh. Well. The point is, feelings don't matter.'

'What?'

'You've got to let Valerie pay for the hospital.'

'Then what is it that matters?'

'What's practical. What happens.'

I was wondering what letters there might be for me at home. I had been away long enough. There was also an unfinished story I had begun about two people on their way to the Dead Sea.

I was becoming overwhelmed by sleep. I dreamed I was in my room at home with the television screen blank. I was on the edge of a salt-imbued sea trying to launch a small paper boat.

When I woke Valentina had gone and Sister Lisa was moving about the room quietly as if not to disturb me. She said 'I'm going to miss you.'

I said 'When am I going?' Then 'I've been dreaming.'

'I know. You've been making noises.'

'What sort of noises?'

'Sort of singing noises.'

'I was trying to launch a paper boat on the Dead Sea. That's what Israelis and Palestinians should be trying to do.'

'What?'

'Finding out if it turns turtle.'

'I don't think you're fit to travel. She must be very fond of you.'

'Who?'

'Valentina. Valerie.'

'Yes.'

'You're not supposed to say yes.'

'Dear Sister Lisa, Mona Lisa, I'm going to miss you too.'

I was thinking – Yes I must get somewhere to be on my own, where no one can come in on me, where I can try to sort out what is happening – no not sort out, that is not possible, but just let it settle, so that the water becomes clear, and one can see the shells, the starfish, on the sand at the bottom; and those strange organisms that stretch out tendrils like the strings attached to balloons, and if you put a hand out to touch them in a flash they disappear. Such might be a setting for fish thrown back into the sea? And for myself, because I am old, and have been all my life creating a tapestry of my mind as if it were the bottom of the sea – not working to a design, no, but the design seems to have been there. But where? In my head? Outside it? That is not an ordinary question because it does not need an answer. In various parts of the world I have watched people – often young girls – weaving cloth which emerges with infinitesimal slowness but with complex pictures and patterns from the loom; and the girls do not seem to work from any model; they are deft, attentive; the shuttle darts to and fro between the strands that open and shut like the mouths of fishes; the process seems to be running itself and yet to depend on the hands of the operator. And I have thought – that young girl is praying; she is in the hands of God. Perhaps in the plane on the way home with white noise around me I will be both operator and operated, dreamer and dreamed; I will make no decisions except to know that decisions will be made. But I will feel the bits and pieces of my life which were together for a moment at the beginning of the universe and then spread, scattered, went on their way – I may find them coming to make sense again without my being able to pin them down except to see them in terms of what might be needed. So I will be writing not of ineluctable time but of mind, of memory: because it is in mind that there are discovered, invented, connections, meanings; which may be of the same stuff as the universe.

We only know that worlds other than our own exist if we look at the night sky in the dark.

7

It was through her daughter Cathy that I had first met Valentina, whose child Cathy was by her first husband. At this time I had been married to Valerie for some twenty years; we had ebbed and flowed on not-too-dangerous tides; then suddenly it was as if I were going over Niagara. I will write of this occasion later. But what has come up now in my mind as a result of Adam's visit to me in the hospital in New York, and his mention of Cathy, is my first meeting with Cathy and Valentina.

I was on my own in London at the time: Valerie had gone to California, where she was gaining recognition for her painting. We were not divorced, and there was not too much acrimony, but I had ceased to have much contact with her. We thought we should get on with our lives, Valerie and I.

I had taken to going for long walks in the summer evenings – for something to do; to keep my mind afloat in the pool at the bottom of my Niagara. My dreams of giving to people a new way of seeing things were in abeyance: my life seemed cast inextricably in the style of a sex-and-betrayal novel. I had given up my post at Oxford, and had no plans for the future. But by this time I had the idea – it is no good planning; a debacle may just have to be endured before one is offered a vision of the future.

On one of my walks on which I seemed to be getting no closer to an ever-receding destination I noticed a small girl standing at the head of a queue at a bus-stop. She was no more than eight or nine; she appeared to be on her own; people behind her in the queue were eyeing her suspiciously; she was keeping them at bay with an air of hauteur and self-sufficiency. This was a time when there was much talk in the media of children being abducted and abused and even murdered; so it was considered something of a crime for grown-ups to let small children be out on their own. But it could be imagined to be the beginning of a crime if anyone offered to help them.

It was getting dark. The small girl, whom I did not yet know as Cathy, did seem vulnerable in spite of her composure. There was a middle-aged woman in the queue who looked as if she were stirring herself to make some move to talk to her. I thought – But then the girl may run and so will not catch her bus. I had not been wanting to take a bus but I found myself joining the queue. I thought – To be responsible means risking being taken for a paedophile.

The middle-aged woman turned and said to no one in particular 'She shouldn't be out on her own.' I smiled. I thought – Perhaps I will be found guilty of trying to pick up a middle-aged lady. When a bus arrived the girl went up the steps but then seemed to have no money to give to the driver: she spoke to him and waited. The people behind her were becoming impatient. I pushed my way to the head of the queue and went up the steps and held out some money to the driver; he seemed reluctant to accept even the responsibility of taking it. The girl looked up at me and said 'My mother will pay you back.' I said 'Oh that's all right.' The driver said 'Are you with her?' But he took my money, and the girl moved to a seat at the back. She was a sturdy little girl with straight brown hair. I followed her down the inside of the bus taking care to pay no more attention to her. I was thinking – But even that may look suspicious: we live in an age when people feel they gain identity by being suspicious.

The bus set off in the opposite direction to that in which I had been heading. I imagined – A magical mystery tour, with or without a police presence at the end! There had been a man sitting in a parked car near to the bus-stop talking into a mobile phone. I wondered – Is it an instinct for guilt that makes one paranoid, or paranoia that gives one guilt?

I was having such fantasies at this time because of the incident which I have mentioned and with which I had become involved not long before. This had concerned a girl considerably older than Cathy, but still one with whom my teacher-pupil relationship had given rise to some scandal. I wondered now – I am trying to make some demonstration about not being affected by that?

The bus had not travelled far before the small girl got up and stood by the door. She had taken no notice of me since I had paid her fare. I nevertheless had the impression that she expected me to follow her; had she not said that her mother would pay me back? And should I not see whatever fancy I had embarked on through to the end? At the bus-stop we were approaching there was a woman in a dressing-gown and with tousled hair; when the bus stopped the girl got off and went up to her and they embraced. I followed the girl out of the bus. I thought – The woman is her mother; she is extraordinarily attractive; it looks as if she has just got out of bed. She said, speaking to the girl but looking at me, 'Your father telephoned to say I must meet you because there was a man who followed you onto the bus.' The girl said 'Yes he paid my fare, and I said we'd pay him back.' I said 'Yes, but you don't have to pay me back.' The woman said 'Why didn't your father pay your fare?' The girl said 'Because he was drunk.' The woman was looking at me as if she were slightly dazed. She said 'I was in the bath.' I said 'Oh that's all right.' The girl said 'He can come back to the house if you haven't got your money.' She set off down a side-street. The woman and I followed her. I thought – We are her puppets with wires to our centres of gravity. The woman called after the girl – 'How did you get rid of your father?' The girl said without turning 'I said I'd scream.' The woman said to me 'It was her father's day for meeting her at school.' I said 'I see.'

We came to a small red sports car parked in the side-street. The woman went to the offside and faced me across the roof. She said 'My husband and I are separated.'

I said again. 'I see.'

'I want to send her to a school in the other direction, so it won't be so easy for him to meet her.'

'Where might you send her?'

'There's a good church school some distance away, but you can't get in unless you're a churchgoer.'

'Well that shouldn't be a problem.'

'It shouldn't?'

'No.'

'You wouldn't have to believe?'

'You'd have to believe that you wanted to get her into that school.'

She stared at me. She said 'It's odd how everyone wants to get their children into a church school yet no one wants to believe.'

I said 'Yes isn't it.'

The girl whom I knew later as Cathy was feeling in the pockets of her mother's dressing-gown. She found some keys and unlocked the offside door of the car and got in and sat in the driving seat. She put a key in the ignition and turned it and the radio came on with loud music. Then she leaned across and opened the passenger door by which I was standing. Then she climbed over the front seats and squatted in the small space at the back.

The woman said 'Which way were you heading?'

I said 'Nowhere particular.'

'Then you'd better come along.'

'Thank you.'

She climbed into the driving seat and turned the radio off. I got in and sat beside her. She made no move to start the car. She said 'But wouldn't that be hypocritical?'

'No.'

'Why not?'

'It would be practical.'

She drove a short way up the street and then stopped in front of a semi-detached house. She said 'What did Cathy's father mean when he said you were following her?'

'I wondered if she had money for the bus.'

'And that was being practical?'

'Yes.'

Cathy stretched forwards to open the passenger-seat window. She began to slide out of it past my ear.

Her mother said 'Cathy's father isn't a bad man but he drinks.'

'I see.'

'Are you married?'

'Yes, but we're sort of separated. My wife's in California.'

'But I wouldn't be able to go to church because I'm too wicked.'

Cathy had done a somersault out of the window and a handstand on the pavement. She now righted herself and put her head back in through the window. She said 'Mum you're not so wicked.' Then she set off down an alleyway at the side of the semi-detached house.

Her mother shouted after her 'You haven't got the keys!'

Cathy didn't answer. She disappeared round the back of the house.

The woman said to me 'Do you believe in that stuff?'

'What stuff?'

'The lost sheep, the prodigal son.'

'Oh yes I believe that.'

'What else?'

'I think I know that church school. We looked at it for my son.'

The front door of the house opened and Cathy was standing inside. She watched us until her mother began to get out of the car; then she disappeared back into the house.

The woman went across a small front garden and I followed. She said 'I wanted a child.'

I said for what seemed the hundredth time 'I see.'

'Cathy's father was at least much better than the previous people I was with.'

'Right.'

'One of them made pornographic films.'

'Did he.'

'I was in one.'

'Were you.'

I thought of saying – I'd like to see it sometime, but I didn't think things had got quite as far as that yet.

The woman was going into the house and I was being drawn along in her wake. She said 'Why am I telling you all this, do you know?'

'I'm not sure.'

'Do you want to be?'

'Yes. Though I'm not sure one ever really is.'

We went down a passage past a sparsely furnished front room; then on to the back where there was a kitchen with tables and chairs and a sofa and a television set. Cathy was lying on the floor on her front and was manipulating the remote control. She said 'Mum, you're being boring.'

'I'm not.'

'You are.'

'Well why shouldn't I be.' Then to me 'Would you like a drink?'

'Yes please.'

'Help yourself. I don't drink.'

I went to a sideboard and poured myself a whisky. I sat on the sofa, and then had for not the first time the experience of being suddenly overwhelmed by sleep. Cathy's mother went out of the room and I heard her going upstairs. I thought of saying – Oh don't bother to get dressed! On the television there was a film about a girl and boy on the back of a dragon. I was thinking that if I fell asleep I would spill my whisky which might give a bad impression, but I did not seem to have the strength to put it down. I must then have fallen asleep because when I woke I was trying to remember what I had been dreaming: something about not knowing where I had parked my car in a strange town. I was lying sprawled on the sofa and someone had taken the whisky from my hand. Cathy and her mother were having a discussion. Her mother was saying 'He can sleep in your room.' Cathy was saying 'Why can't he sleep in yours?' Her mother said 'You can come in with me.' Cathy said 'You usually have such boring people!' I was keeping my eyes closed. I thought – I might seem to be dreaming, but I'm not.

Cathy's mother was saying 'How do you know he isn't boring?'

'Because he paid my fare and didn't try to talk to me.'

'Why do you think he followed you?'

'I suppose to get off with you.'

'But he didn't know me!'

'Perhaps he thought he did.'

'Well all right, he can stay on the sofa.'

'Oh all right, he can have my room. I'll sleep on the sofa!'

'I've only just met him!'

'So why were you telling him all that boring stuff?'

'You wouldn't understand.'

'Saying that is so boring! You thought it would impress him.'

'Not the stuff; perhaps the fact I was telling him.'

'Then explain.'

'I wanted to get it over with.'

'Finding out if he was boring?'

'Yes. And having to tell him. You're not supposed to understand!'

'Well I don't.'

'Yes you do.'

'All right.'

'Are you listening?'

The last remark was by Cathy's mother and seemed to be addressed to me. I opened my eyes and said 'Yes.'

'Well what do you want to do?'

'I want all decisions made for me.'

'Then sleep on the sofa.'

'Yes I think that's best.'

'Cathy's going to bed.'

Cathy said 'We haven't had any supper.'

I said 'I'll take us all out to supper!' I sat up.

Cathy's mother said 'No, I think we've had enough excitement. And there's stuff in the fridge.'

While she was bending down to look in the fridge I said 'What made you stop?'

'Stop what?'

'Drinking. Doing that film.'

'I suppose having Cathy.'

'That was clever.'

Cathy said 'Brilliant.' Then to me 'Have you got any children?'

I said 'One. A boy. He's called Adam.'

'How old is he?'

'Thirteen.'

Cathy's mother said 'A bit old for you, but he'd better watch out.'

Cathy said 'Now you're being boring again!'

I said 'I think this is the least boring conversation I've ever had!'

Cathy's mother said 'Well now you tell us what were you doing wandering about at the bus-stop.'

Cathy said 'Give me a plate and I'll take it up to bed.'

8

After years of working at an Oxford college I had begun to feel atrophy settling into my veins. Oxford was an institution dedicated to the evolution of an intellectual tradition, but evolution as well as tradition required that for the most part species stayed the same. Only occasionally would a mutation be allowed to take root – at the cost of what had before seemed valuable.

The days had long since gone when dons had had to be ordained members of the Church of England, but with the idea of the death of God taking root, what authority was there for any tradition? Rationality became enthroned; and in a discipline such as mine, anthropology, this meant that any idea might be honoured that could be argued and presented cleverly. And in literature what could most easily be seen as entertaining were stories of human silliness or squalor – though approbation was still given to humour. But if frivolity became too bold there were the restraints of political correctness.

I had liked to teach that it was art that had meaning. Indeed what was art except that which had meaning, and what was meaning except that which was conveyed by art? But these ideas were self-reflecting; they did not step outside their cocoon to exhibit proof; either someone saw the point of them or they did not. And meaning implied a message (this idea was deeply unfashionable) even if the message could not be put into precise words. But if watched, or listened to, a work might convey its message. And if this proposition was said to be meaningless then this was its message – a modern intellectual mutation was that there was no meaning, no message.

There were a few maverick voices that might, or might not, become part of a new tradition: one of these, I had once been arrogant enough to hope, might be mine. I argued against meaninglessness and political correctness: I recommended exploration, and trying things out. But I became discouraged: I could so easily be made a fool of! And I was not yet confident enough to make a virtue of this. My relationship with the college, the university, became ever more tenuous. I was thinking that sooner or later I would have to get out.

I had begun to appear occasionally on television, where I could ride my hobby-horses. I would say – But humans do not like peace, they are at home in war: they cannot stand happiness, they require resentment and complaint. There was for a time a demand for this sort of thing; but I needed to extend my repertoire if I was not to become a bore.

In the course of my reading I had come across traditions in which frivolity and convention did not seem to be a prevailing fashion. In particular I became interested in certain sects, tendencies, in the part of the Middle East that had once been Persia and was now Iran. Here were celebrated the teaching and style of old Persian poetry and mysticism; in this messages and recommendations were conveyed not through injunctions but through stories; and the stories were open to interpretation. The interpretation depended on the interaction in the reader or listener between the poetry and his own life. One message that was conveyed was that if an individual wishes to be in touch with virtue he has often to be in opposition to prevailing conventions and laws; and if as a result he has to endure censure and hardship, then this may be what is required for a receptive state of mind. He may have to welcome, that is, becoming something of an outcast or a clown. And those who stick to established paths are likely to become rigid with arrogance or complacency. In the locality in which I was interested this tradition had been largely overrun by militant Islam; but it flourished in individuals and in villages in the hills, and the hostility it evoked ensured its purity and thus even its survival.

I had been led to this information by Barbara, an anthropologist in a neighbouring college. Barbara had taken the place of Tom in my life as the person with whom I liked to chat in the pub on my way home in the evenings. She was slightly older than me and was divorced; but we kept off the subject of personal relationships. We gossiped about work in a vaguely flirtatious way, but Barbara did not seem interested in disturbing my marriage to Valerie.

About my hobby-horses she would say 'You're too parochial. You take your ideas about what's going on in the world from what you read in the papers.'

'But they're what form our view of the world.'

'Why not rather – They're the absurd cover under which we can get on with our own relationship with the world.'

'That's what your Persians do?'

'Yes. Why not come and join me there and see.'

'When are you going?'

'I'm taking a sabbatical at the end of the year. I mean just come on a visit. Don't get me wrong!'

'No I won't get you wrong.'

Although I was not interested in making a pass at Barbara,

I had been thinking that there should be more chances of adventure in a not-often-visited part of the world, and I was in need of adventure. Valerie was in California, and I was becoming accustomed to the idea that she might be settling into an affair there.

I said to Barbara 'But these people in the hills, what do they think of Western decadence, Western imperialism; and the terrorism of militant Islam?'

'I don't suppose they think of them much at all. They keep their heads down.'

'And they manage this?'

'Yes.'

'And go their own way?'

'Yes.'

'Look, I really might love to come.'

Barbara was going to look into what might be the origins of the myth of the Garden of Eden. There were various theories concerning the geography of this: in a corner of north-western Iran for instance there were correlations between the biblical descriptions and the landscape. But it was not so much the Garden of Eden as the style of the people known as Sufis that I had become intrigued about – their intimations about how to stay alive and flourish in a hostile world.

Before Valerie had left for California she had been talking about Adam possibly being better off in boarding school. And if I went to Iran, this would become necessary. I felt I should sound Adam out about this. He was now a tall, serious boy of thirteen; he had a way of gazing at me when I talked as if he were trying to follow a foreign language. I said to him 'You'd be better with children of your own age. You're so much on your own here.'

'I like being on my own.'

'And sports! You'd be able to do sports!'

'I don't see the point of actually *doing* sports.'

'The rough and tumble of life! All that rubbish.'

'Yes as you say that's rubbish.'

'But look, I may be going on a trip: to Iran, and you can't stay here on your own.'

'What's Mum doing?'

'I suppose she'll still be away.'

'Then why didn't you say so? All right, I'll go to a boarding school.'

'I'm sorry.'

'I don't see the point of actually *being* sorry.'

I thought – But he is more sad or angry about his mother than about me.

I said 'I know we're selfish, Mum and I, but at least we don't pretend we're not.'

'It's the pretending that's the rubbish?'

'I think so.'

'Yes that's what you say.'

I thought – You actually remember what I say?

So Adam went to a boarding school, and I prepared to visit Barbara who was now already in Iran.

Barbara had lent me books about the old Persian attitudes to religion, one of which was a long poem written in the twelfth century called *The Conference of the Birds*. This was like an extract from a Persian Old Testament, and seemed to me to make more sense than the Koran. *The Conference of the Birds* told the story of the birds of the world getting together to try to discover what they were here for: they put themselves under the tutelage of the hoopoe bird, who undertook to lead them on a journey. On their journey they would become stripped of the burdensome accoutrements of the self, and would become ready to meet God.

When Barbara had described to me what the poem was about, I had said 'But isn't there a contradiction here?'

'How?'

'You say it advocates being both detached and passionately committed.'

'Yes: not either/or but both/and.'

'The best of both worlds? Then that's the stuff for me! I'll send you a carrier pigeon when I'm coming.'

I telephoned to Valerie and said 'Adam seems to be all right at school. I'm off to Iran to have a mystical experience.'

'Do you mean with that woman called Barbara?'

'Yes.'

'Well have a good experience as they say in California.'

'Try to get back before too long for Adam.'

'Didn't you say he was all right at school?'

'Yes.'

'All right then.'

I had not paid all that much attention to the political situation in Iran. These were the last days of the rule of the Shah; fundamentalist Muslims were trying to seize power, but their brand of aggression was not yet being exported. Barbara had gone out with the hope of finding her mythical Garden of Eden: I was hoping for a physical as well as a spiritual experience.

Just before I left I got a postcard from Barbara saying that the area she had intended to explore in the north-east was now dominated by chemical works, with flames belching from chimneys like the sword of the angel preventing return to Eden. So she was moving to a village somewhat to the south, which might be more like the garden that Adam and Eve had had to create after they had been banished from Eden.

In the course of my journey to Iran I read *The Conference of the Birds*. The journey of the birds was long and arduous; it was by odd encounters that the accretions of the self might be cast off. One of the ways by which this might occur, the hoopoe bird had said, was by coming across, yielding to, being ravaged by, an overwhelming but impossible love for another human. Thus one would be humbled, cleansed; and at the end of the journey one might come face to face with the God that was – one's true Self!

I thought – Well never mind the humiliation, that's the God for me.

I had wondered at moments how Barbara saw her role in this. I was aware that she might after all have become slightly in love with me; but this did not seem a threat to what we had talked about and planned.

When eventually I arrived at Barbara's village – via a modern airport, a modern city, in which crowds eddied not with the aimlessness of a Western crowd but purposeful with brandished fists as if looking for doors guarding heaven to batter down – there was a long valley with fruit trees between green and blue mountains; a settlement of low mud-brick houses that seemed to have grown from the earth. Here men sat around and smoked and talked; women went to and fro in cloaks and shawls or were just visible through doorways surrounded by pots and pans or drinking tea. In the distance boys ran with sheep and goats in the hills. There was harmony; but no impression that people were trying to reproduce Eden. It was as if they knew they might have to be on the move again.

So how was I to pass my time here? About field-work anthropology I had once written – It should be recognised that what an anthropologist is doing is not simply studying an unfamiliar society, but observing the reactions of people who find themselves observed by an intruder.

I thought now – Perhaps an anthropologist might even be interested in the function of himself as intruder?

I asked Barbara if she could arrange one or two interviews for me. She said 'But anyway you didn't come here just to work.'

73

'Why do you think I came?'

'You said you wanted to get away.'

'Yes. But that's a cliché.'

'The reason why men usually want to get away is sex.'

'Yes but that's also a cliché.'

'You'll have to watch if you don't want to get it chopped off here.'

I wondered – Perhaps after all Barbara has designs on me.

The sexual customs of the village seemed on the surface to be in accordance with strict Islamic law. Marital fidelity was expected and enjoined on the part of wives, with threats of dire retribution for transgression. Regarding men, both expectations and injunctions seemed deliberately enigmatic: law was a matter of words; its practice was tempered by the understanding and mercy of Allah. For unmarried girls sex was totally taboo, but it seemed that a certain coquetry was not discouraged. From the carefully arranged shawls that covered heads, bits of faces would peep out roguishly; it seemed accepted that men might be tempted. I was briefed on all this by Barbara, who added that there were a few older women who seemed available to young men on condition that this was not talked about; condemnation would be not so much for behaviour as for display; like this it was possible that both morality and immorality could be given their due. I said to Barbara 'Just like upper-class Edwardian England!'

She said 'Speak for yourself.'

'I think it's brilliant.'

I thought – That was a mistake; but I am getting somewhat rattled by Barbara.

She said 'You think those upper-class Englishmen ever thought of sex as anything but purchase and power?'

'Yes.'

'What?'

'They were liable to put women on pedestals like goddesses.'

'From which women couldn't get down to be fucked by anyone else.'

'But they could if they were married.'

'And you call that morality?'

'No, I call it trying to get the best of both worlds.'

Barbara offered to get me an interpreter so that I could interview some of the old men of the village. I said I would rather wander about and see what I could find on my own. Barbara said 'Or would you rather I fixed up some interviews with young girls?'

I said 'Barbara, you're being difficult.'

'I didn't know you'd be so bashful.'

'It was you who suggested I come here!'

'You do what you like.'

I did carry out one or two interviews. The old people watched me as if to find what I wanted to hear. If they could not divine this – perhaps because I did not know it myself – the interview was likely to peter out, with me perhaps trying to explain what I was doing.

I thought – But where is the spirituality that is supposed to be going on under the cover of this conventional world? I do not see this because I am thought to be representative of the hostile world?

There was one young girl whom, as soon as I had noticed her, I began to look out for in the street. I could hardly tell if she was conventionally beautiful since I got so few glimpses of her face. But she had a way of moving, of being in repose even, that went straight to my guts, heart, mind: it was as if she herself were some image that was locked inside me and was demanding to be liberated: but this would involve tearing my own guts, heart, mind. I thought – But is not this what I have come here for?

When I came across this girl in the street she did not coquette; she kept her eyes cast down. In my fraught condition this seemed to hint more at intimacy than flirtation. I dreamed that I might arrange to interview her on the grounds that she might be someone to give me straight answers. But what would be my straight questions?

She had a routine of going at a certain time each evening past the bungalow at which Barbara and I were staying; she carried a bucket and a bundle of washing and seemed to be on her way to the stream that ran at the side of the village. As I became more obsessed by the vision of her (was not this what was recommended in *The Conference of the Birds*?) I began to feel that she might be performing her evening routine know-ingly – knowing, that is, that I would be on the verandah of the bungalow waiting for her and watching. But Barbara was sometimes on the verandah too. One day the girl was late.

Barbara said 'She's not coming today.'

I said 'Ah.'

'Didn't I tell you all you men are the same?'

'Barbara, I might as well say all you women are the same.'

'She comes this way to fetch water.'

'I think it's to do her washing.'

'Why don't you have a go with me? I'm pretty good.'

'That's very kind of you Barbara.'

'Kind!'

'I mean dashing, romantic.'

'I'm just letting you know I could do with a fuck.'

The girl appeared. She was carrying her bucket and her bundle. Inside her long garment her body seemed to flow like liquid and yet hold itself miraculously together. It was as if her garment might be ready to shed itself like the skin of a snake. I thought – She must wonder what's going on here: I hope she's getting it right. She went on down a path towards the stream.

I said 'Barbara, that would fuck up our friendship.'

'You mean you don't like me.'

'Barbara you know the rules—'

'What rules?'

'One does what one can, for God's sake!'

'How sanctimonious can you get! Our friendship's already fucked.'

I left her and set off down a different path towards the stream. I wondered – Will Barbara betray me to the fundamentalist Islamic police? Send an anonymous letter to Valerie? But what has happened is that I have been given a push towards the stream.

I found the girl kneeling over the water; she had taken the shawl from her head and shoulders. I thought – Oh dear God, this is a fork in the road of existence and I will be haunted to death unless I take a chance!

I said 'Hello.' She said 'Hello.' I said 'You understand English?'

'Yes I learned it in school.'

'Where was that?'

'In Tehran.'

'I wonder if I could ask you a few questions.'

'If you like.' Then she said quickly 'I want to come to England.'

I said 'Why?'

'It is not good here.'

'But your family's here?'

She did not answer. I sat on a log at the side of the stream. I thought – Why not cast myself head-first into the water and be done with it.

She said 'Are you married?'

'Yes.'

'Is that your wife with you here?'

'No.'

'Where is your wife?'

'In America.'

'I see.'

'But we live in England.'

'In London?'

'Yes.'

'I am sorry, it is I who am asking the questions.'

'No, that's all right.'

I thought – I am on the point of saying – Why don't you come with me to England?

She said 'Of course you can ask me any question you like.'

9

After my first sight of Cathy at the bus-stop and my going along with her so that I met Valentina whom I moved in with, I could well think – None of this would have happened if I had not been wandering in London streets; and I would not have been wandering if there had not been the events with the girl in Iran and their immediate aftermath. And so this is what I mean by things having a pattern of their own if you risk them; you cannot plot them; you can either deny that such patterning exists or raise your hat to it respectfully.

When I moved into Valentina's house the problem of beds was solved by my sleeping with Valentina – which is what Cathy had seemed to be suggesting from the start. This arrangement lasted. Valerie remained in California. As part of Valentina's and my strategy to get Cathy into the more suitable church school we all three took to going to the local church on Sunday. This gave us a function. It was an evangelical 'clap-happy' church, with hymns accompanied by drums and guitar, and the words on a sheet lowered from the ceiling. Valentina muttered 'I don't think I can stand this.' I said 'Watch and wonder.' Cathy laughed and clapped her hands in time to the music.

Then when the news reached her old school that plans were being made for Cathy to leave it to go to the more classy school up the road, she came in for a certain amount of bullying. I said to Valentina 'Talk to the headmistress.' Valentina said 'Isn't that supposed to make things worse?' Then one evening I found Cathy with a stencil set she had been given at Christmas laboriously printing on the front of one of her T-shirts I AM A POSH CUNT. I said 'Are you going to go to school wearing that?' Cathy said 'It's what they call me and that's what I am.' Valentina said 'It's the school photograph tomorrow!'

It seems that Cathy turned up at school with a denim jacket over her T-shirt and then just before the photograph was taken she was told to take the jacket off and so she did, and the picture was taken with the slogan visible. The photographer made proofs without apparently noticing anything unusual, and sent one to the headmistress. When she saw the slogan and Cathy looking belligerent she assumed that Cathy must have been forced to wear the T-shirt by her persecutors. The whole school was threatened with the loss of a holiday unless the culprit or culprits owned up. Cathy declared that she had printed the slogan herself, but she was not believed; it was thought she was covering up for her fellow pupils. Cathy stuck to her story. No one knew what to believe: but in the end no one was punished, and the bullying stopped.

I said to Valentina 'She's a genius! You're lucky with Cathy.'

Valentina said 'Well so are you. But do you think they'll have her now at the church school?'

'Of course they will! They'll be thrilled. They'll be rescuing a lost sheep.'

So Cathy went to the church school: and there was even a story – probably apocryphal – that the headmaster had thought of using the incident of the T-shirt in one of his sermons, but was dissuaded because the point he would be making would be too enigmatic.

The first time Adam met Cathy was at a half-term weekend from his boarding school. Valerie and I were in the process of giving up our home in Oxford, so I had told her that of course I would be responsible for Adam at half term. But then there was the question of whether he should come to Valentina's, or whether I should take him to a seaside hotel. Valentina said 'Of course he must come here! Are you afraid he'll be embarrassed?'

I said 'No I'm afraid he won't be.'

'Well that's pathetic! You won't be embarrassed, will you, Cathy?'

Cathy said 'Yes I'll be embarrassed.'

'All right he needn't come!'

Cathy said 'He can have my room.'

'No, we'll fix up a camp-bed in the front room.'

So Adam came, stepping warily into the hallway of Valentina's small house and carrying nothing but a comb and a toothbrush I had bought him at the station. Cathy was standing at the entrance to the kitchen ready to greet him: Adam saw her, paused, then swerved off into the front room where I had explained he was sleeping. When Valentina came to greet him he answered politely but kept his eyes turned to the floor. I thought – Can it be true even of Adam that children find unbearable the thought of their parents having any sort of sex?

We all went out to dinner that night and Adam was still paying no attention to Cathy. To cover up a silence Valentina began to tell the story of Cathy and the school photograph; but when it came to the punchline of what was on the T-shirt she dried up. Adam said 'Well what was on it?' Cathy said 'I am a posh cunt.' Adam looked at her for what seemed to be the first time and said 'Oh that was brilliant!'

Later Valentina said 'But I still think he has bad manners.'

'I don't think he cares much about manners.'

'I suppose his mother thought herself too aristocratic!'

'Yes she's a posh cunt.'

'Oh aren't you all clever!'

I said 'I think Adam's a bit in love with Cathy.'

So Adam came to stay in the holidays in Valentina's house; and then sometime later during his last year at boarding school he himself became implicated in a case of bullying. A boy had become unpopular because he was said to be a show-off, a braggart – a bit of a bully himself: he had been taken off by his classmates and given some sort of ritual beating. Adam had not been active in this but he had known about it and been in a position of responsibility, and had apparently done nothing to stop it. The boy had told his mother, who had complained to the headmaster, and those involved had been sent home and told they could not return to school until further notice. I said to Valentina 'They call this a punishment?' Valentina said 'I think it's what's called paradoxical therapy.'

'You reward people for doing wrong so that they feel guilty?'

'Something like that.'

'Does it work?'

'It's not been tried much.'

When he arrived at Valentina's house Adam said 'I can stay with a friend if it's inconvenient.'

Valentina said 'It's not at all inconvenient. You can help clear the gutters on the roof.'

I rang up Valerie and she said 'But you must talk to him! Bullying's terrible!'

I said 'Yes. Or it might be a chance for things to become better.'

'You never do talk with Adam. You just try to be clever.'

When I thought about this it seemed to be partly true. But was not parents' laying down the law a form of bullying? Or was it that parents were frightened of learning from their children?

I found a time to talk to Adam. I said 'Well did you or didn't you have anything to do with the bullying?'

He said 'Oh well I knew it was happening.'

'And you didn't do anything to stop it?'

'Oh well, if I hadn't been around, it might have been worse.'

'Did it make the boy any better?'

'Oh well, he'd been asking for it in a way, and I think he quite wanted it, actually. Yes, when it was over, I suppose he might have felt better.'

I thought – You talk as if you were God!

I said 'But did the people doing the bullying like it?'

'Oh well, people think they do, don't they? It's like television. But I don't know if they do really.'

'Did you watch it? Did you like that?'

'Oh I wondered if I might, but I don't think I would, actually. And I think the others stopped when they saw the boy might be liking it.'

I was thinking – More like Proust than God.

I rang Valerie in California to tell her of this conversation. She said 'Is Adam kinky?' I said 'No, he may be clever.' She said 'And the rest of us are not?'

I said 'The world's kinky.'

My conversation with Adam had taken place in Valentina's kitchen. I had realised that Cathy was probably listening. I thought – Perhaps we have all got something to learn from this.

Then, later, I overheard Cathy talking to Adam in the room which was Adam's bedroom. She was saying 'But did he say he was liking it?'

'No he couldn't really say that, could he?'

'Not even to himself?'

'Well he might, but then he might have stopped liking it.'

'But that would be a good thing, wouldn't it?'

'Yes I see that.'

I thought – But what on earth is happening here?

Also – If Adam and Cathy are so clever so young, might they one day help to stop the world being kinky?

Valentina came down the stairs and said 'What on earth are you all on about?'

I said 'We were talking about why people like being beaten up.'

We all gravitated into the kitchen as if we were a jury requiring further instruction before we gave our verdict.

Adam said 'The thing is, the boy was pushing drugs. Everyone knew this. The headmaster knew it. That's why we were only sent home.'

Valentina said 'But why on earth hasn't anyone said this before?'

'No one asked.'

I said 'It's the sort of thing that no one would want to come out.'

'But that's disgraceful!'

'It's a wonder it's come out now.'

Then Cathy said 'That's the sort of thing my father wanted to do with me.'

Valentina said 'Push drugs?'

Cathy said 'No, punish me.'

I said 'What for?'

'Anything. It didn't matter. He felt so guilty.'

Valentina said 'What? But this is terrible!'

Cathy said 'He was so miserable.'

'And that's why he wanted to punish you?'

Cathy said 'Yes, but it's not the same thing.'

84

Adam said 'You mean he beat you?'

Cathy said 'It was only a game!'

Valentina said 'I'm going to ring him up!'

Cathy said 'If you do I'll never tell you anything again.'

I said 'I thought he's doing a cure in that detox place.'

Cathy said 'I think he wanted to punish himself.'

Adam said 'And that made him better?'

Cathy said 'He didn't really hurt me.'

Valentina said 'Are you all insane? I don't believe this!'

Adam said 'That's because it's interesting.'

I said 'But is it true?'

Cathy said 'No, all right, it's not true. I made it up.'

Adam said 'And I made up the thing about drugs.'

I said 'Well there we are then.'

Valentina said 'Will you all please all shut up! Just shut up!'

So we hung around in the kitchen having an interesting time not looking at each other, and being glad to have got it out but now to shut up.

Neither Valentina nor I wanted at the moment to question Cathy further about her father, but I said I thought it best if I rather than she looked for an opportunity to talk to Cathy later.

By this time I had got a view of Cathy, and indeed of Adam, as the sort of children that we had once been told to become like if we wanted to get into heaven – both innocent and knowing; without hang-ups or guilt. But did grown-ups need to feel guilt?

When the chance arose one evening I said to Cathy 'Can you tell me a bit more about what you got up to with your father?'

'Why do you want to know?'

'Well of course I do. But hardly anyone likes to talk about that sort of thing because it's too difficult.'

85

'You won't tell Mum? You'll keep it secret?'

'Yes.'

'Well when he picked me up from school he used to say he was suicidal.'

'I see.'

'He said – Help me, can you help me.'

'Yes.'

'So we used to play a game—'

'Yes.'

'That I'd been naughty—'

'Which you hadn't—'

'No. But that's what cheered him up.'

'Because he could punish you?'

'As a game. Yes.'

'But he didn't hurt you?'

'Not really.'

'Did you mind?'

'Not much.'

'Did it make things easier for you?'

'Oh I see. Well he was my father. I couldn't bear him to be so miserable.'

'And it did cheer him?'

'It seemed to. It seemed the only thing I could do for him.'

'And so did you feel better?'

'In a way, I think so. But I sometimes wondered, because afterwards, yes, he'd feel so guilty.'

'But he was guilty—'

'Yes. He was so ashamed.'

'Cathy, this is so dangerous! Even if it may be how things work.'

'How?'

'I mean if people get things out. If they can see them. They can change.'

Cathy had begun to cry. I had not imagined Cathy crying.

I said 'Cathy don't cry! You did nothing wrong! You were wonderful!'

'I wanted to save him and I don't think I did.'

'You can't in the end save other people. But perhaps you did!'

'You mean in the end everyone has to save themselves?'

'I think so. Yes.'

'He's gone into this home.'

'Yes. Perhaps you made him see things. See himself. He may get better.'

Cathy had stopped crying. I wondered – Did that thing in heaven mean that children are angels, or both angels and devils?

She said 'Have you ever done anything like that?'

'Like what?'

'Done something stupid or wrong for yourself or another person.'

I said 'Oh well, yes. But I always thought I was doing it for myself.'

'What? When?'

'But also someone I was able to help. Yes.'

'Tell me.'

'Perhaps I will one day.'

'Why not now?'

'Because it's too difficult. I don't know the outcome yet. But you should probably trust it, yes.'

10

I had begun to try to recollect, assimilate, to imagine into a shape which would offer meaning, these memories and experiences, while Valentina was making arrangements to fly me back to London from New York. I had talked with Cathy; the occasion in my own story I had mentioned but had not wanted to go on about had a background of which I did not know at the time, which I would discover later. But would there not always be things to become apparent and to be learned later, and so on to infinity?

And where was it that I imagined things were being sorted out? In one's mind: but thus also in the outside world.

When I had rejoined Barbara on the verandah of our bungalow she said 'I'm sorry for what I said.' I said 'That's all right Barbara.' I was thinking – Barbara might hold the balance between one sort of disaster and another in her hands.

I had said to the girl by the stream – I'll fix an interview.

The girl had said – Yes do. She had gathered up her washing.

I said to Barbara 'It's I who am sorry.'

Barbara said 'That girl is what one might call assassination-bait.'

'Who might they kill, her or me?'

'Both, probably.'

I was thinking – Would I mind?

'They seem such peaceable people!'

'Assassins can come from anywhere.'

I was recalling this on my last day in New York. I wondered – How about that man who ran me over in the van?

Valentina completed the arrangements to fly me home. While we were waiting at the airport with myself in a wheelchair Valentina said 'Well you'd better tell me what you've been sorting out about yourself.'

I said 'I've been wondering if you'd ever be interested!'

'Well I've asked, haven't I?'

'You remember that girl you used to say might be a terrorist?'

'Oh not her!'

'Well she wasn't, but she did induce a sort of paralysis. You know that poem I've told you about – the poem about the birds? And one of the birds suggests that when the chance comes you should risk everything for an obsessive love?'

'But not lust.'

'Well, whatever. The point being – how else do you escape from the traps and trappings of your past.'

'Well not by making a fool of yourself.'

'Why not?'

'You destroyed your marriage.

'Or I wouldn't be married now to you.'

'But you chose that.'

'I don't know. When I saw Cathy at the bus-stop I was sleepwalking.'

'You mean if it hadn't been for that Iranian girl you'd still be happily married?'

'Well, not happily.'

'You could say that about anything – If it wasn't for this or that, we wouldn't be where we are now.'

'Well that's true, isn't it?'

I went back to trying to remember what had happened after I had rejoined Barbara on our verandah. I did not see the girl for a day or two: she did not come down to the stream. I wondered if her family might have heard of our conversation and locked her up, or stoned her, or whatever. But how could they have heard – unless she had told them? And why should she have done that – unless, oh yes, it was me who was due to be stoned or— or what?

But she wanted to come to England!

I had told her that I would arrange an interview. This would have to be done together with her family. Also I did not think I could carry this through without Barbara.

Valentina and I had progressed to the first-class compartment of a plane. My leg was stuck out in front of me like a cannon. I said 'But the thing is, should one go on considering something wrong or ridiculous if its effects turn out to be good.'

'I don't think one can argue that retrospectively.'

'No, but you can see it. Everything's connected – here and there, forward and back. That's the experience.'

'Look, I really don't want to hear about your wonderful old love affair just now.'

'No, but there it is.'

Barbara had gone about her business in the village. And in fact her attitude to me seemed to be becoming less disapproving. She said 'What do you know about this girl's family?'

'Nothing.'

'It seems they're good people.'

'I was wondering if I could get an interview with them.'

'But look, what is it that you want with her? Apart from the obvious I mean.'

'Barbara, I don't know. She said she wants to come to England.'

'I suppose they all want to do that.'

'Yes.'

'But look, those old poets you're so keen on, they weren't giving practical advice. Poetry's a metaphor.'

'I suppose so.'

'You know that.'

'But what's a metaphor?'

'Well I'll see what I can do. About an interview I mean.'

'Barbara, you're an angel!'

'How do you know I'm not a scorned woman luring you to your doom?'

'I wouldn't care.'

'Yes you would.'

Barbara located the girl's family and asked if I could interview them. I could not make out what Barbara was up to; but I did not worry. I learned that the girl was called Nadia.

Her family lived in a brick-built house with an inner courtyard from which steps went up to a large room on the first floor. Here an elderly man, whom I took to be Nadia's father, was seated on an imposing chair like a throne. Four young men stood around him: I thought – These are Nadia's brothers or cousins, who if I lay a finger on her will kill me. An old woman sat motionless in the shadows. There was no sign of Nadia. I had been told that the father and possibly one of his sons understood English. I said 'It's good of you to talk to me.'

One of the young men said something in their language that I did not understand, but which seemed to be a reference to Allah.

After a time of the usual questioning and answers about customs and society, I found myself saying 'But do you wish life in the village, in the family, to go on as it has always gone on, without change?'

The elderly man had been watching me intently as if to catch a glimpse of what might be at the back of what I was saying. I wondered – But is this not what I have wanted? He now turned to one of the young men beside him and they conversed briefly in their language. Then he said 'There is nothing in the Koran that prohibits learning.'

The young man to whom he had spoken said 'So long as it is on the path to God.'

I said 'Yes indeed.'

The old man said 'You have spoken to my daughter?'

'Yes.'

'I thought – So what has Nadia told them?

I was getting the impression that we were talking not at cross purposes but even with parallel purposes. I had intended to get round to suggesting that Nadia might come to England to further her education; that I could be responsible for her if she did this. I was not being entirely duplicitous, because I knew that Barbara had contacts with a scheme that got students from the Middle East to places in European universities. And had not Nadia asked me to help her get to England? What I had not expected was that her family seemed to be so much in collusion with this.

Through a window I glimpsed Nadia crossing the court-yard. She was approaching the steps which led to the room in which we were sitting. I felt that this scene, as with my previous meeting with Nadia, was getting, as perhaps it always had been, wildly out of my control. But what did this matter: I would be in the same room with her!

I said 'It is important that young people should want to learn more about a changing world.'

One of the young men said 'it is also natural that their families should wish to protect them.'

I said 'Quite.'

The elderly man said 'Allah is not against learning.'

Nadia had entered the room and she sat on a seat by the window. She opened a book she had been carrying and started reading. It looked as if the book was in English. She had arranged her shawl down around her shoulders.

One of the young men said 'It is sometimes necessary for people to go their own way.'

Another said 'Even if the world is against this.'

The first said 'Especially if this world is against this.'

I said 'That is true.'

I thought — If there is something going its own way here, then we should stop talking. Of course there was something relevant to my own obsession, but there seemed also to be something in the family's hopes and fears that they could not talk about, but which they were trying to convey to me. I realised — Even if Nadia has told them about her telling me of her wish to come to England, and even if they agree with this, they might still have to deny it — to feel free to safeguard both themselves and her from what traditionalists in the village might make of it. But I did not want to work out too much about this, because things were going along so remarkably.

The old woman was muttering something from the shadows. There was a short exchange between her and one of the young men. I gazed at a corner of the ceiling. I thought — This is what communication in that tower must have been like before it became Babel.

After a time the elderly man said 'We have a saying — He who knows God's will becomes silent.'

I said 'Yes I believe that.'

I saw that Nadia was looking at me. She said 'I am told that you are a professor of English.'

I said 'Yes. Of cultural studies.'

'Could you teach me?'

'I can take you to where you can be taught.'

'Will you do that?'

'I must talk to the lady where I am staying. You know where that is.'

'Yes.'

'She may be able to make arrangements.'

I thought – Now say nothing more. There is nothing more to be said.

The other people in the room seemed to be acknowledging this.

I got up to go. I bowed. I did not look at Nadia. I had felt that after the interview I would go for a long walk in the hills, but I soon began to worry that I had not said enough to Nadia.

I found Barbara on the verandah talking to one of the old women of the village. I said 'Barbara, I must talk to you. I don't understand what's happening!' The old woman, without looking at me, got up to go.

I said 'Barbara, I think Nadia's family want her to go with me to England.'

She said 'Of course they don't.'

'Well tell me I'm crazy.'

'You're crazy.'

'Nadia told me she wants me to take her.'

'You want to fuck her.'

'Yes. No. Of course I do. But that's not the point.'

'What is the point?'

'Something's going on. Being worked out. I don't know.'

'For God's sake, is that your technique? Do you ever get round to fucking anyone?'

'Yes. No. I don't know. What are they up to? Why do they want her to go?'

'Look, if you want to take her, don't inquire into things too closely.'

'Well I agree with that. But what things?'

I suddenly thought – What does Barbara know? What has that old woman been telling her?

I went down to the stream to see if I could bump into Nadia. Of course I might be walking into some sort of trap. If I knew this, should I not want to get out? But I didn't.

How old was Nadia? Was she under age in England?

If I could make love to her just once, might it be over?

But not here. It was true she might be killed if it was here.

But did I think I could settle down with her in England?

It seemed to be true that my marriage to Valerie was over.

But this was madness. Perhaps it was nothing more; and when it came to it I would not want to fuck her.

Nadia was not by the stream. In the poem about the birds, the one who was in love became like a madman, rolling about and weeping.

I went back to the bungalow. Barbara wasn't there. I thought – She is out and about making more inquiries in the village? When she came in I said 'Barbara, have you got any tranquillisers?'

'For temporary alleviation or for suicide?'

'Either. Both. One risks it.'

'I've got some whisky.'

'Barbara, you're being an angel. Why don't I fuck you?'

'Daft humans don't fuck angels.'

'Is that so? Perhaps Nadia's a devil.'

'Indeed. Do you know how old she is?'

'No, do you?'

'They say she's sixteen. But she might be less. Or possibly more.'

'What exactly did that old woman tell you?'

'Nothing. She said nothing.'

'Do you think the family could be infiltrating one member into England so that the rest can follow?'

'No, you don't think that. But as you do know, I've got contacts with this student organisation and I could probably get her into England. I could say she needs asylum. That her family are in danger. Which God knows after this they might be.'

'Barbara, why are you doing this?'

'I told you, I might be ruining you. Getting a permanent hold over you.'

'Can I have some more whisky?'

'Help yourself. I'll have to give your name as vouching for her.'

'Of course.' I thought – Then I might have some permanent hold over Nadia?

Barbara said 'Have you thought that it might be her who is using you?'

'Of course. But Barbara, there's something you're not telling me.'

'I think you should leave here now. Go home. Don't see her again.'

'What is it? Everyone's playing a game? Bluffing? I might be in danger?'

'That's what I'm telling you.'

'Yes. I mean no.'

'All right, I'll see if I can work it. I'll let you know.'

'Barbara, you're crazy!'

'I hope I'm not being unfair.'

'Unfair!'

Then someone was saying 'Why are you smiling?' But this was not Barbara, but Valentina, who was sitting beside me on the plane that was taking us home to England.

11

Sometime after I had retired from teaching and before I had gone to America and was playing the role of a gadfly to the ox of political correctness on radio and television – Adam and Cathy were grown up by this time and Valentina and I were married and had moved to the house in north London with the basement where I worked – I read of an exhibition, or entertainment, which was being held in the subterranean level of a large public building in London. In this, members of the public were being invited to experience what it was like to be blind. Several interconnecting spaces were kept in darkness; those who had come to sample the event gathered in a waiting-room in the light. There they – or rather we, because one day I got myself to attend – sat in a gloomy silence as is usual in England when strangers are cast together; we took care not to catch one another's eyes. I suppose we felt we were engaged in a form of childishness.

Our guide or mentor appeared – a woman who was truly blind. She explained that we had to choose a leader; then to form a crocodile holding on to one another as we proceeded on our journey into the dark. We would find simulated such experiences as blind people have in the world; we would hear street noises, voices, sounds of traffic, dogs; we would have to interpret these – so as not to trip, become lost, get run over. Eventually we would come – having learned by touch, by imagination, by intelligence, to find our way – to a pub or café where we could order drinks and sandwiches, still in the dark. I, because I was by far the oldest in our group and already carried a stick, was chosen as leader. I set off, tapping, with the hand of the person behind me holding on to my jacket, and so on down the line.

One effect of this experiment was that almost as soon as we had set off our group, who in the light had resisted any friendliness, became alert, chatty, almost giggly; we swapped information and conjectures and jokes up and down the line – Oi! What's that! Edge of the pavement? Coal-hole! We had become dependent on one another; with myself as leader even feeling a responsibility to keep my followers cheerful by making them laugh. So after what seemed a hazardous journey, by the time we reached the pub we felt ourselves to be on terms of goodwill and jollity if not exactly of intimacy; however, groups who had arrived before us at the pub were lingering so genially that our mentor told us that we would have to wait outside until there was room. I wondered – I should be learning patience too? But by this time I was eager to be on my own – to be able to ruminate on this experience and perhaps to write something of it down. I told our guide that unfortunately I had an urgent appointment and would have to go; she led me to an exit. Later I wondered – Don't I want to be cheerful in a crowded pub?

What was being learnt, it seemed to me, was that to find one's way in almost any circumstances one had to inquire, to question, to keep an open mind, as if one were in the dark; it was in the light that one reacted automatically according to prejudice and easy assumptions. But still, one did need often to be alone? In this technological age one was bombarded with information and opinion which made it difficult to think: as with people under torture, it was easiest to say whatever seemed required. But one could be in conversation with oneself?

It was thus that I had come to like watching television with the sound turned off. In parallel with the blindness experiment it seemed that it was the faculty of speech that bedevilled humans and left them prey to programmed reactions; sounds battered the brain even more relentlessly than light. With sounds turned off humans could see themselves needing, striving, often failing to make sense or contact; but failure could then be seen as something that they might put right.

In the great big outside world during these days there was war and atrocity in the Balkans; the impression of people making determined stands against the chances of harmony. Perhaps in reaction to this there were one or two television presenters, mostly women, who seemed to want to make out that at least they were on terms of goodwill with their audience; they would joke, cajole, flirt with them almost; turning with eyes cast down and then looking up wide-eyed into the camera as if saying – Look, we know, don't we, you and I, that these current-affairs programmes are for the most part dismal; and we know, don't we, you and I, that there's a demand to watch ghastly things; but why should we get downhearted about this? We can still make something personal and pleasant of the fact that we know about it, can't we? and let the world go by. So here am I: how are you?

Then one day a woman reporter appeared who was serene and humorous and who did not flirt, but who gave to me the impression that I must know her in real life – might have been on quite intimate terms with her in fact, though I could not place her in memory. Then it dawned on me – like the emanation of a ghost floating through a wall – that she was someone – or exactly like someone – whom I had been with recently in a dream – one of those nostalgic, romantic dreams that elderly men are sometimes lucky enough to have and which (for me at least) did not now have much to do with sex but still provided the heart-warming pleasure of dalliance, of embracement, with the assurance of further meetings being possible. And now here she was – my inamorata – in one of the trouble-spots of the world (Bosnia? Jerusalem?) sending me messages – coded of course and even wordless – telling me just by her presence, her appearance, not to worry, she and I at least were all right. And it was perhaps inevitable that in my imagination I felt as if she might be some emissary from Nadia.

I said to Valentina 'I had a dream of someone the other night and now I've seen her on television!'

Valentina said 'Lucky you.'

'Of course it's possible I'd seen her on the telly before my dream and had forgotten, but it seemed the other way round.'

'Yes it's nicer for you the other way.'

'Why aren't you therapists any longer interested in dreams?'

'You can't pin them down. You can make of them what you like.'

'But isn't that the point? They're out of your control.'

'But then how can you use them?'

'You find out what you like? You can wonder if they're using you!'

I saw my presenter several times again on television when she was reporting from Kosovo and Macedonia. And because I had travelled myself in this area a few years before – having become interested in the early Christian monasteries in Serbia and the style of their frescos which were of warrior saints rather than of martyrs – it did seem to me that my reporter and I were communicating with one another by a system that might embrace, all right, electronics as well as imagination and dreams.

Then there was an occasion not long before I went to New York when I was asked by the BBC to be interviewed for a radio programme on the subject of the spread of terrorism, with emphasis on what the attitude of the individual might be to this. My contribution would be recorded and broadcast later.

In the BBC building I was led through corridors to a box-like room where there was a table with two microphones and two chairs and a glass wall beyond which was the room where the producer operated the sound controls. And sitting at the far side of the table facing me was my television presenter. She glanced at me for a moment as I came in; then looked away. She said 'I'm so glad you could do this, I've wanted to meet you.' I said 'I've wanted to meet you too.' I sat down opposite her. I thought – But this is happening in a reality system, not an alternative one. She said 'I've been reading some of your stuff.' A voice, presumably the producer's, came through a speaker from the next room – 'Can you keep talking please; we're testing.' My presenter said 'You wrote a piece about how you were travelling once in Kosovo and were visiting a monastery which was later destroyed, and a young nun, without knowing you, handed over to you for safe keeping one of their most treasured possessions, a tapestry of Saint Isidora.' I said 'Yes, I had the impression that the nun felt she must know me in some sense, even though we didn't speak each other's language.' My presenter said 'And later, after the monastery had been looted and burnt, you sold the tapestry and handed over the considerable sum of money it raised to a fund for bringing Kosovo orphans to this country?' I said 'Yes, I felt that this must be what she had wanted.'

'And there were no repercussions?'

'No.'

The voice of the producer came from the next room – 'All right now, thank you, we're ready.'

My presenter said 'Yes I went to that monastery some time after you, and there was not much left of it.' She looked down at her notebook.

I thought – How are we going to talk in a manner that is not intimate.

She said 'I'm interested in other things you have written; about how there do seem to be alternative networks to what is called reality; what Jung called synchronicity.'

I said 'Yes, but Jung made the mistake of trying to present them as scientific.'

'But they are experienced.'

'It does seem so, yes.'

She looked up at me and there was the impression again of spirits walking through walls. She looked down quickly at her notebook.

The voice of the producer came over the speaker – 'Have you two lovebirds finished yet?'

My presenter said as if reading from her notebook 'You have spoken of the folly of imagining that the effects of something like a pre-emptive strike in war can be rationally assessed: there is no way of foretelling the future.'

I said 'One can have a go I suppose at assessing probabilities.'

'But not do much about them?'

'Well, one can keep a look out.'

'And that's rational?'

'Oh yes, I think so.'

'But also humorous.'

She kept her head down. There was a long silence. I had the impression we were pinned in some no man's land.

I said 'Well, in the style we've both been talking about.'

She looked up. She said 'You mean, and there's then just what happens?'

The head of the producer appeared round the door of our room. He said 'Do you want us to be recording this?'

My presenter said 'No.'

I said 'I don't mind.'

The producer disappeared.

My presenter said 'Have you heard what happened to those orphans you helped to bring here from Kosovo?'

I said 'No. But there are no reports of their becoming a menace or a burden.'

'But even if there were?'

'Yes – so what.'

There was another long silence. Then she said 'There's another story I want to ask you about.'

I said 'Yes?'

The voice of the producer came over the speaker – 'Look, we're going to need this room in ten minutes.'

My presenter said 'All right, scrub it.'

The producer said 'You want me to scrub the interview?'

'Yes. You always scrub anything that's interesting anyway.' She closed her notebook and put an elastic band round it. She stood up. She came round the table. She said to me 'Or is there anything else you particularly wanted to say?'

I said 'You look like Saint Isidora.'

'That's a very nice thing to say.'

The producer had come to the door and was holding it open for us. He said 'I didn't know you two know each other.'

She said 'We don't.'

I said 'Oh yes, we do.'

She said 'Oh yes, so we do.'

I said 'Can I give you a lift?'

'I'm afraid there'll be a car for me. I've got to catch a plane this evening.'

'Where to?'

'Bethlehem. Jerusalem. But I can give you the number of my mobile.'

'Yes will you do that?'

We were halfway along a featureless corridor when we realised we had not said goodbye to the producer. We turned, but he had gone. She said 'Oh well.'

We went on to the lift. I said 'What was the other story you wanted to ask me about?'

'You know that girl you brought back from Iran?'

'How on earth do you know about that?'

'What happened to her?'

'I don't see her. I think she's all right.'

'And were you?'

'All right?'

'Yes. I mean there was a bit of a row, wasn't there? Did it hurt you?'

'Only in a way that was all right.'

We had come to the doors of the lift. We were waiting for it to arrive. She was facing me but not looking at me, and smiling. She said 'You gave up Oxford—'

'Yes.'

'And your marriage. You didn't mind that?'

'Oh well, I minded.'

'But you didn't stay with her. With the girl I mean.'

'No.'

'Why not? No, not why not. Did you manage it?'

'Manage it!'

She started to laugh, and put her head against my shoulder.

The lift arrived. There is something unsettling anyway about two people alone in a lift: emanations, images, bounce off walls like trapped energy.

She said 'I mean, when you'd got her to England, you might have felt that that charitable deed precluded anything else. But I've always hoped it should be possible to have the best of both worlds.'

I said 'Yes it is.'

'It was?'

'For a very short while. Yes.'

'I'm so glad.'

'But look, how do you know about this?'

The lift stopped and some people got in. My presenter and I became like people who do not know one another. When the lift reached the ground floor we remained like this while people got out and others waited to get in. Then she said 'This is my mobile number, will you ring me?' She handed me a card.

I said 'Yes.'

We moved out of the lift. She said 'I expect to see Cathy in Bethlehem.'

I said 'Cathy? You know Cathy?'

'Yes. Didn't she tell you?'

'No.'

'I expect she was shy.' Then 'How else do you think I know so much about you?'

12

When I arrived back in London from New York I settled into my basement chair with my leg propped up in front of me and I did not want to go back to being hooked on television: I wanted to try to catch, to put on paper, what had been sparked off and gone on in my mind in America and on the journey home. I had been saying for years that the sort of interactions, connections, in which 'truth' might reside, could not be pinned down; but I wanted to try to express how these intimations slipped out of one's grasp but were yet there, like fish with enormous eyes at the bottom of the ocean. I had been remembering my meeting with my television presenter: she had evoked memories of Nadia; then unexpectedly of Cathy, with whom I had lost touch. If there were intended connections here that could not be pinned down, I could nevertheless look for them.

I dug out of a drawer some pages that I had written years ago just after my time with Nadia. I read –

The feeling that I remember when I finally arrived with Nadia in our hotel room in the north of England was fear – a sort of metaphysical fear, such as a pillager might feel when stepping into a holy of holies; such as those women were said to have felt when they came across the empty tomb. (If this is blasphemy, so be it.) I was stepping across a threshold into a potentiality for explosion; the atoms and molecules of heart and mind might disintegrate, dissolve; I myself would have been the engine of destruction. In such a situation the usual fear is that one will not get an erection . . .

I thought – Oh God this is terrible stuff! No wonder I buried it. I read on –

. . . but would an erection here be that terrible tower that led to the collapse into Babel? I remember Nadia saying in the car – we were on our way to a hotel not far from the university to which I would be taking her in a day or two – You will be good to Barbara, won't you; she has been very good to us. And I was thinking – Perhaps I will crash the car and be delivered from the terrible tyranny of love and genes. I was doing what I felt I should not do, what it seemed even now that I did not really want to do, what at the same time I felt I must not stop. This might have been the predicament that had struck St Paul when he noted that Jesus saved sinners: he had commented – Should I therefore sin that grace may abound? And had answered himself – God forbid!

I thought – Well, for God's sake, God forbid! But God hadn't.

And then I saw that I had scribbled in the margin – '*Perhaps I just wanted to get it over with so that grace might abound?*'

I thought – But that's not blasphemy!

My telephone made its inharmonious jangling sound. I was sitting in my chair with my leg in front of me like a battering ram. Then at the other end of the electric impulses was Cathy. She said 'Every time I get back to England I fear you may be dead.'

I said 'Well I nearly was.'

'I know.'

'I've been hearing about you.'

'I know.'

'What do you mean you know?'

I tried to remember my conversation with Adam (or was it Valerie or Valentina?) in New York. But before that there had been my conversation at the BBC with my television presenter, in which she had said something about Cathy being too shy to tell me – what? It had not been clear.

Cathy said 'I want to come and see you. Are you presentable?'

'I'm always presentable.'

'I mean I don't want you to be in terrible distress or horribly disfigured. I want to talk about myself.'

'I always want to talk about myself.'

'I'll be with you in twenty minutes.'

My television presenter had been talking about Nadia. She had wondered if I had managed to make love with Nadia. She had heard the story of Nadia from Cathy. She had come across Cathy in Bethlehem. What was it about Bethlehem? Oh.

Cathy came bounding into my basement long before the twenty minutes were up. I thought – She must have been speaking on her mobile phone from just outside in the street. Then – She moves like Adam.

I waved the pages that I was holding and said 'I've been looking at something I wrote about what you wanted me to tell you about years ago but then I couldn't put it into words and it still doesn't seem I can. But what do you want to talk about?'

Cathy said 'You used to say I liked playing God.'

'Oh yes. We'd been talking about your father.'

'And whether one can sin so that grace may abound. Well, my father wasn't too bad before he died.'

'So that was all right.'

Cathy looked older than when I had last seen her. She was now – what – thirty-one, -two? And Adam was – thirty-five, -six? But Cathy seemed ill at ease, tongue-tied. So I went on 'But what I've been wanting to ask you is, have you seen Adam recently?'

'Oh yes, he's been in America hasn't he?'

'And you've been back to Bethlehem.'

'How did you hear that? Oh yes, from that person who I suppose is one of the people you behaved disgracefully with so that grace might abound.'

'What person?'

'She's called Tania. She's a television presenter.'

'But I've never behaved disgracefully with her!'

'Oh haven't you? She seems very keen on you. She wanted to know all about you.'

'You're changing the subject.'

'Yes, if we get in enough muddle perhaps you'll drop it.'

'But you were in Bethlehem before. You went back.'

'I've been back to Bethlehem and then Jerusalem.'

'Have you heard about Adam's wanting to adopt a baby?'

'Well now isn't that just the most completely against all conventional and moral principles thing you've ever heard!'

I said 'Cathy!' Then 'I see.'

'What do you see? You're always saying you see, and then you never say what it is.'

'All right tell me what happened in Bethlehem.'

'It was where Jesus was born, didn't you know?'

'Yes.'

'All right. There were all these people holed up in the Church of the Nativity. The Israelis had surrounded it with tanks and guns. There were said to be terrorists, suicide bombers, inside, as well as refugees. Is that what you wanted to hear?'

'I don't know. Go on.'

'Do you think Jesus was a suicide bomber?'

'No.'

'But isn't that about playing God? Isn't it morally acceptable for everyone to be wiped out so long as that includes wiping out oneself?'

'Are we talking about morals?'

'All right, what's required is something new.'

'A baby's something new.'

'Is it? It could be. Perhaps one has a right to think it could. But it didn't work that time, did it?'

'You don't know.'

'Well did it? You mean it might be working even if it doesn't seem to be?' Cathy seemed to be on the edge of tears.

I said 'Go on with the story.'

'Well the Israelis weren't storming the church because that would be bad for their image. The people inside the church were said to be starving and dying, but that could be good for their image. So there was a stand-off. My lot were ready to rush food and medicine to the church but the Israeli commander said he couldn't be responsible for our safety. We said we didn't want him to be responsible, we didn't mind dashing across the square and getting shot because that might be good for our image. But then someone who was supposed to have been inside the church said there weren't in fact people starving and dying there, it just suited everyone to keep up these appearances in order to keep the business going.' Cathy broke off. She had been walking up and down: now she stopped with her back to me. She said 'Someone did say there was a pregnant woman in the church but I don't know if that was true.'

I thought – You mean, you might have a better story? About a different sort of baby?

I said 'Go on.'

'Then your friend Tania turned up with her film crew. The Israelis thought they'd be hostile to them, so they only let them film the architecture. Bill the cameraman said he wouldn't mind us running across the square and being shot because he might win an award if he got a picture. But Tania and the Israeli commander had by this time made friends; they were wondering if it would be best for everyone's what's-the-opposite-of-an-image if this sort of routine went on for ever. I mean it gave them a sort of identity. Though no one could say this, because then the warfare would look ridiculous. I asked the Israeli commander if he knew the story of the Nativity, and he said yes, but did anyone believe it? I said that wasn't the point; it was a good story.'

Cathy broke off. After a time I said 'And what did Tania say?'

'She said it might be a better story that the Franciscans and the Armenians from the monasteries next door to the church were in fact keeping people alive by sending in food and medicine. I said – But no one wants to hear this. The Israeli commander said – And if they knew they'd think they had to stop it. I said – But what if there was a new sort of baby that no one quite knew about? That needn't have to die. Tania said – How would you manage that? I said – Well, it shouldn't be too difficult.'

I said 'And what happened then?'

'Well eventually we did get into the church because one of the Armenians struck a deal with both sides on the understanding that it remained secret. Things in the church were not too bad. There were no decomposing bodies.'

'But was there a baby?'

Cathy seemed to be crying quite silently. She said 'I didn't want to bring a baby into this god-damn awful world, where everyone wants war and hatred to go on because what would people do without them.'

I said 'But Cathy, you're not like that. You're good.'

She said 'And let it be crucified!'

'All right, don't talk about it. Let it just happen.'

'No one wants to change. And if people are happy in the shit, then let them be.'

'But not you and Adam.'

'No, not me and Adam.' She turned and faced me. 'So why doesn't he get angry with me?'

'Doesn't he get angry with you?'

'No.'

'I suppose he knows that's not what works.'

'He wants me to do it by myself.'

'Do what?'

'Come round to him. Agree. Both care and not care. So we can't take it out on one another.'

'Well that might do it.'

'Do what?'

'Produce a sensible baby.'

She had stopped crying. I realised that I had only once seen Cathy cry as a child, when she had talked about her father. I thought – But as a mother, one can cry?

I said 'Where is the baby?'

She said 'What baby?'

'All right. But things can change, even human beings, if there are enough chances.'

'But there aren't. All Tania wanted to talk about was that girl who you fucked, where was it, in that tower going up to heaven or somewhere.'

'I thought you said you thought that was Tania.'

'Oh yes I did, didn't I.'

'You make your own chances. So what are you going to do?'

'Nothing. I'm going to do nothing. I'm going to sit still.'

'That might be a sensible thing to do.'

She appeared to look for a handkerchief; then she wiped her hands on her jeans.

She said 'Adam's been talking to you, has he?'

'Yes.'

'And he's coming back soon?'

'So he says.'

'The clever brute.'

'And then you'll see him?'

'Yes I'll see him.'

'Good.'

I cannot remember what happened next, because I fell asleep. This was what often happened to me nowadays. There used to come into my head the quotation about 'Sleep that knits up the ravelled sleeve of care' – or was it 'unravelled'? No. I was more 'ravelled'. And then I was waking up some time later.

Cathy had gone. I thought – I probably know as much about what is going on as is required.

I thought I should try to get through to my television presenter on the number of her mobile phone that she had given me weeks ago. I tapped away and was transferred to an answering service. I left a message to say that I had called: then I tried to go back to sleep. I thought of another quote, from a philosopher – How do I know what I am going to say until I say it?

Tania rang back quickly. She said 'Are you all right? I heard you'd been run over.'

'That seems a long time ago. I sometimes wonder if I arranged it.'

'I was kept up to date by Cathy.'

'Yes, she's been here. I want to ask you — has she been having a baby?'

'You make it sound like the measles.'

'She made it sound like an asteroid that's going to wipe us out.'

'Are you cross she didn't tell you?'

'No. I should have rung you earlier.'

'Weren't you holed up in New York?'

'Yes. But I mean, was Cathy's plan to have the baby actually in the Church of the Nativity, or after she'd been shot rushing across the square?'

'Something almost as glamorous.'

'But not so different—'

'Oh I think so, definitely.'

There was a long silence. I became anxious lest she think I had rung off, so I said 'Are you still in Bethlehem?'

'No I'm in Jerusalem.'

'What are you doing there?'

'Oh looking after the baby for God's sake!'

'You mean literally?'

'Oh when has anything ever been just literal!'

'Yes. Quite.'

'Adam's on his way out here.'

I thought – You know about Adam? Yes, of course. I said 'Cathy says everyone's beginning to accept that the war will go on for ever.'

'Which might mean that out of boredom one day it will stop.'

'Yes I see that.'

'Has Cathy ever remotely done any of the things that normal people do?'

'I can't think of any, no.'

'But it's OK.'

'Is it?'

'Yes.'

'And then will Adam be coming back here?'

'I think so.'

'Well I'm very grateful to you. Really.'

'Oh I say, jolly good. J. G. That's what we used to say at school.'

I thought this was the right moment to ring off. And I wanted to go back to have a look at the bit of story that I had been reading before Cathy rang. I wondered if I really felt it so pretentious. I read again – '*Should I therefore sin so that grace may abound? And had answered himself – God forbid!*'

I had written further –

When Nadia and I got to the hotel it suddenly seemed as if it did not matter whether or not we made love. She said 'We don't have to go through with this you know.' I said 'Oh well, I think we do.' She said 'You're very good to me.' I said 'I'm good to you!' When we made love she at first lay quite still while I crawled over her like clouds above a landscape. Then towards the end she uttered a great cry as if she were giving up the ghost, or embracing one.

13

When I did start watching television again it was as if the world or this way of presenting it might be seen in a new light. Humans had always been saying that things were not right as they were; that they wanted change. But now it seemed to be dawning on people that perhaps after all they did not want change, so dependent were they on saying that things were not right as they were. The stories they liked to hear about were of duplicity and corruption in public life; in personal life of tragedy and desire for revenge. What distinguished humans from animals seemed now to be not so much intelligence and language as the compulsion to accuse, to blame, to complain; to demand retribution and compensation. This was now being accepted as a customary way of life; why should there be responsibility for change?

Crowds drifted or revelled as if in the last days before Armageddon. What better was there to do, if there was no wish for a different future? There had always been a dark attraction about self-destruction: now it seemed purposeful, rational.

Some time ago I had begun to write a story about two people, an orthodox Jew and a newly converted Jewish

Christian, who were escaping from Jerusalem at the time of its destruction by the Romans in AD 70. On their way from the burning city they talked; they agreed that the present calamity was God's retribution for human wrongdoing; the one maintained that there was little that humans could do about this because God was all-powerful and ineffable; but the other claimed that by becoming human God had made it clear that humans were responsible for what went on upon earth. In the course of their argument the two had taken a wrong turning and had come not to the coast where a boat might have taken them to Alexandria, but to the shore of the Dead Sea. They stared at the thick and oily water that appeared itself about to catch fire like the burning city behind them. One was saying – But how can God be God if he is not all-powerful? The other was saying – What sort of God is it that just wants power? But this one agreed that God would have to have the power to make human freedom and responsibility possible.

I found the beginning of this story among the papers that I dug out after my return from America: I had not known how to go on with it. Should my two characters try to get across the Dead Sea and into the desert where they might find – what? – a location for a new start beyond quarrels about words? Should they look for, or set about building, a boat like Noah's Ark? Should they try to swim? Was it true that swimmers turned upside down in the Dead Sea?

I was wondering what to make of this on the evening of the day when Cathy had been to visit me. Valentina came in and said 'Do you know how hot it is in here? You haven't even opened your window!'

I said 'Do you know if people turn turtle in the Dead Sea?'

'Has Cathy been round here?'

'Has she been in touch with you?'

'I think she wanted to make sure I wasn't in.'

I had the television on with the sound off. Subtitles slithered like snakes across the lower bodies of people holding forth. America was becoming an imperialist oppressor, Russia had become a capitalist cornucopia, anyone in the Middle East was a potential suicide bomber, the British were interested only in fashion and snobbery. The people in dispute seemed to be tickled by the subtitles into laughter. I wondered – What subtitles would slither across Valentina and me?

She said 'You should go out more. You watch too much television.'

I said 'The streets are teeming with murderers, muggers, paedophiles and suicide bombers.'

'The doctor said you can use your crutches.'

'Like Samson with the jawbone of an ox.'

'I've got a lot of evening meetings this month. I want to know that I can leave you.'

'Yes, you can leave me.'

'Then you can get up to no good if you want.'

'The average Englishman thinks of sex about once every four minutes.'

'I thought it was seconds.'

I was thinking – But people do change! Valentina has become one of those strong, confident women who should be taking over the running of the world, and probably are. So aren't I lucky.

There was an organisation called the Dining Club of which I was a member. This was a self-elected body of men only that met for dinner once a month to continue the sort of talk they had been involved in during the day. They were politicians, journalists, civil servants. I had welcomed becoming a member because I thought I might learn from the serious debates between people who thought they were running the world; and I could put on a display which might be amusing even if I made a bit of a fool of myself. But as things were, people rattled on like an orchestra whose members all need to make the one effect; and there was no demand for people to make fools of themselves. Valerie had once commented – But that's your way of showing contempt. I had said – I thought it showed humility. She had said – Same thing, probably.

However, one evening when Valentina was out I dragged myself off to the Dining Club thinking that at least I might be able to spin an amusing story about why I was on crutches; also might there not be someone there who would know the effect of the salinity of the Dead Sea? But then when I appeared on my crutches it was as if I were a threat to the flock like a bird with a broken wing; and how could I explain my interest in the Dead Sea? So there was nothing much for me to do except to drink the rather good wine and make one or two provocative remarks about the uproar of orchestral music. I thought I might add this to my repertoire of hobby-horses – the idea that music mugged the mind's ability to learn, and left it prey to the totalitarianism of emotions.

There was a member of the Dining Club called Henderson who was known as a senior civil servant, but because his job was never quite defined he was also rumoured to be some high-up in the intelligence services. He was an imposing man with silver hair who seemed to have been groomed so he would look like someone high up in the intelligence services, and so – what – one wouldn't be taken in by this? At the end of this dinner there was an empty chair beside me and Henderson came and sat in it. He said 'What's your connection to Charlie von Richtoven?'

I said 'I don't think he's really "von". He's my first wife's lover.'

'I see. Well what do you think of his idea that people in the Middle East want to lure more and more American troops into the area so that they will be a protection against nuclear retaliation when Al-Qaeda have another go at blowing up New York?'

I said 'You mean that they, whoever they are, are encouraging the Americans to invade not only Iraq but also, say, Syria or Iran, so that—'

'Got to have some deterrence against the deterrent if you haven't got your own—'

'You mean that then the Americans won't drop a nuke, or whatever they call it, on wherever it might be, so that then they, the others, whoever they are, can get on with their plans to get the present appalling American administration re-elected by blowing up New York?'

Henderson smiled and said 'I have not said that!'

I said 'That's brilliant!'

'I thought you might have some good ideas.'

I thought – This is an amazingly interesting conversation because there are almost infinite possibilities about what it might mean.

I said 'They'd have to have their bombs already in place in suitcases in New York, so that then they could blame the Americans for doing it themselves—'

'Which they do anyway—'

'So the Americans might as well do it themselves—'

'And get themselves re-elected?'

'And of course blame the others.'

He smiled and turned away.

I thought – What I really wanted to ask him about was whether people turn upside down in the Dead Sea.

Then he turned back to me suddenly and said 'I wondered if you and your wife would like to have dinner with us some time.'

'Yes we'd love to.'

'My wife thinks she knows you. She met you somewhere abroad.'

'Oh did she?'

'She says she'd like to see you again.'

I thought – Barbara? He must be married to Barbara!

I said 'Yes I'd love to see her!'

I began to have a conversation in my mind with Valentina. There's a madman in MI5 who thinks I may have intelligence information or something about what is going on in the Middle East. Valentina was saying – Well that's the sort of impression you like to give when you're drunk.

Henderson had turned away again. I went back to thinking of what to do with my Jew and my Christian at the Dead Sea. I would have to make it clear that it was right that they had taken what they thought was a wrong turning because if they had got to Alexandria, which they had wanted to do, history would have continued with endless boring repetitions as in fact it has done—

Perhaps the paper boat that they sailed on the Dead Sea might contain the message – Do you not see that you each depend on the other?

But had I not at some stage thought of getting them to pick up a baby on their way to the Dead Sea?

Henderson had turned back again. He was saying 'You're with your second wife now, aren't you?'

'Yes.'

'Then she shouldn't mind if I ask my wife to get in touch with her.'

'No I'm sure not.'

I wondered – Why on earth should she mind?

Valerie might have minded Barbara?

Or was it just that this conversation was like one in the pre-Babel tower – with chatter not orchestrated so that everyone had to be trying so hard to make out what anyone, including themselves, was meaning.

When I eventually got home I said to Valentina 'There's a madman in MI5 called Henderson who's going to ring up and ask us to dinner.' Valentina said 'Were you drunk?' I said 'Not very. I think he must be married to Barbara.'

'I thought you were trying to avoid Barbara.'

'Yes, but I shouldn't have been.'

'Come on, I'll help you to bed.'

I said 'I think Henderson might think I'd been to bed with Barbara. But I hadn't. Can you remember?'

'No.'

'It was important that I didn't.'

'Was it.'

'I don't know if she's his first or second wife.'

'Look, I'm going to bed.'

By the time we went to dinner with the Hendersons I had an image running through my mind of one's perception of reality as a sort of cinema show: I was the projectionist and for most of the time the director, but I did not think I played all that big a part as scriptwriter or producer because scripts and logistics came ready-made from the world outside. At the moment I was trying to make of life a witty comedy-drama; but studios nowadays put up money only for violence or farce. So what would I make of the Hendersons? Who in fact was his wife? If she were indeed Barbara, would he not be requiring some alternative script to *Othello* – because he realised I had not been to bed with his wife rather than he thought I had? I had always thought that *Othello* would be better as a farce.

Anyway to be a successful director, I told myself, one had to have meticulous control of alcohol intake on the set. I had been sipping whisky up to the moment we set off for the Hendersons: I hoped they would run the sort of establishment that would have a maid with a tray of drinks in the hall. Thus, without a gap in intake, one might handle either tragedy or farce.

But it was Henderson himself who greeted us in the hall, and there was the boring stage-business of what to do with one's coat. Through an open door I saw a table with bottles and glasses laid out: there was a man standing by this however that I thought I knew but could not quite place; I hoped he would not accost me before I got to the table. I was introducing Valentina to Henderson but I realised that I did not know his Christian name: I thought a way of getting round this might be to make out that I couldn't remember Valentina's name – this sort of thing sometimes raised a laugh. The man who had been by the drinks table was coming towards me smiling; perhaps I should make out that of course I remembered him! so that there would not be all the boring business of not remembering him and then no delay in getting to the drinks. He said 'I heard you'd been run over.' I said 'Yes I was.'

'How did it happen?'

'Oh it was nothing!'

'But you're still on crutches.'

'Oh well, it was something, yes.'

I said to myself – Now don't start on the boring story of it having been a hit by the FBI or the CIA. Valentina was waiting for me to introduce her: I had already begun to make out that I did not know who she was. The man was saying 'You don't know who I am, do you.' I said 'Yes of course I do!' Valentina said 'I'll get you a drink.' I said to Valentina 'You're an angel, you must tell me who you are.'

Then I began to realise that the man I was talking to was my old friend Tom. I had not seen him since the night Adam was born: he had telephoned me just after this to say that he was taking his broken heart off to Australia. He was now rather fat and had little hair; so after all he might not be Tom. I said 'It's an extraordinary human accomplishment to be able to distinguish between faces.' The man who I thought was Tom said 'It's presumably an advantage in evolution.' I said 'Yes, but I sometimes think it would be the mark of a superior civilisation if we couldn't distinguish between faces; after all, most people are much the same.' The man who I thought was Tom said 'Yes, the Chinese find it difficult to distinguish between European faces.' I said 'Ah yes, did you go to China? I thought it was Australia.' I thought – This conversation is so boring that surely evolution will have to strike us dead.

Valentina returned with a glass of champagne. I said 'We're talking about how it might be a more economical use of brain power to see everyone as the same.' Valentina was saying 'I'm Valentina.' The man who I thought was Tom said 'I'm Tom.' I drank half of my glass quickly and then I set off towards the drinks table: I thought – I must not be rendered immobile again. I was having to hold my half-glass upright on the hand-rest of my crutch, which was requiring much skill and concentration. I thought – Perhaps Babel occurs when one is trapped without a drink in one's hand: but with one balanced on a crutch one can still get up to heaven? A woman was offering me a chair. I said 'Thank you, but I'm almost there.' She said 'Where?' I said 'Heaven.' I had reached the table and was refilling my glass; but then one of my crutches slipped and the woman caught it as it fell. She said 'What happened, did you tread on a landmine?'

I said 'No, I got run over.' I thought – Oh God, but I do not think I can stand too much reality. And I have not even looked at her yet.

She said 'You know me?'

I said 'Yes of course.'

'That is your wife?'

'Yes I've married again.'

'Yes, I saw your first wife when she came out of hospital.'

'And are you now Mrs Henderson?'

'Yes.'

'You seem to have grown a new leg. A new evolutionary accomplishment.'

'I didn't have to make a point any more, so I got a proper one.'

'And have you got children?'

'Yes, four. And twelve grandchildren.'

'I'm so terribly glad.'

'Well yes, so am I. I wanted to see you again to thank you.'

'I wanted to thank you too.'

'What for?'

'For teaching me what you taught me.'

'I taught you!'

'Yes.'

'You taught me that I could make love.'

I had not until now looked much higher than her leg. It was almost fifty years since I had seen her. Her face was still formidable, like that of an Egyptian goddess, with one eye humorous and the other all-seeing and all-knowing. I said 'You haven't changed.'

She said 'Oh well you have a bit.'

'How?'

'You've now got your poor leg.'

I said 'I think you taught me what love is.'

14

It was after this meeting that I felt able to try to put into proper words the story that I had not known how to write about before. Words have become so associated with Babel, how do you make acceptable what is not suited to being said?

When I woke in the early morning after my night with Nadia it was as if some protective cladding had been taken from me which had been the habit of explanation and justification. I felt freed from this; but also from the feeling that I had any control. I was in free-fall; at the mercy of space which was nevertheless part of my being.

Nadia was sleeping beside me with her head turned slightly away. If I leaned over her I might breathe her breath and this would be like oxygen at a high altitude. I would not be able to remain for long at that height; only as long as she stayed by me.

I thought – We are Adam and Eve revisiting their bombed-out garden.

What seemed important was that I should watch and breathe, but no longer taste or touch her. This I had done last night: I had climbed, claimed her. How should one wish to reach the summit more than once! Except for suicide.

I might raise the sheet and look at the landscape below: see if there was anything that had been altered from her; except myself.

I would resign from my position at Oxford: there would even now be stories of impropriety. How had the outcome been described in The Conference of the Birds? Accretions had been stripped off; one was face to face with oneself. The accretions had come from playing Knowledge as if it were a game; using cloth-tipped foils and épées so that there would not be blood but stale air from burst balloons.

Nadia rolled over so that I could see the length of her back. If one spread one's wings, could one fly? She stretched out a hand not to cover herself but to see if I was there.

We would go walking this morning in the hills, Nadia and I. We would have to get used to time as a dimension one could move within. The next day I would take her to the college where she had a place reserved for her. Everything was present all at once in eternity.

When Valerie had recovered from her operation on our honeymoon she and I had gone on a journey to see wild animals on the plains. Valerie sat in the Land Rover propped on cushions; we had been advised not to make love. But we were lucky, our white hunter told us, because on our second day we saw a lioness with her cubs just after she had made a kill — of a deer, which appeared to be still alive because its eyes were blinking. It moved to and fro rhythmically as if it were being made love to as the lioness and her cubs pushed and pulled at its guts. I thought — You mean, all physical love is a matter of eating and being eaten. Or is it that fucking is the sustaining but not the making of love?

With myself and the woman with the metal leg — there had been learning about love.

One of the lion cubs had become impatient with the scrummage at the deer's guts; it stretched its teeth round the soft flesh of the deer's mouth. I had wanted to shout — Stick to the guts!

I was leaning on one elbow and looking down at Nadia's mouth. I wondered if when she woke we would have anything to *say to each other ever again. My voice would be so graceless; would crack glass, loosen bricks, cause walls to come crashing down. But was this what we still wanted? We had uncovered views over hills to distant mountains. How much can one bear of reality.*

Nadia opened her eyes and smiled. Perhaps I could try – We can spend one more night here and then I can take you to the college in the morning. Or – Glory be to God! Or – Do you need any clothes, darling Nadia? Or even – Would you like breakfast? I put my head down against hers as if I might rest it against the hotplate of a stove. Or best – We can walk in the hills today, darling Nadia.

I got out of bed and went to the door to the adjoining room that I had booked for the sake of propriety. Nadia called out after me 'Shall I order breakfast on the telephone? I have seen how to do this on television.' I said 'Yes please.' I thought – Well that didn't sound too bad. Then – We have to practise normality if we are to establish the mutation.

While I was in the next room I heard her talking on the telephone. I thought – And I will get used to this terrifying surrender. I wondered if I should wait in the next room till I heard the breakfast arriving: but now, what was propriety? Nadia had got out of bed and was going across our room to the bathroom: she was naked except for the bedspread which trailed behind her like an afterbirth. I thought – I would never get used to this! She called out 'How does this thing work?' She was trying to manipulate the tap of the shower – one of those levers which you pull from side to side as well as forward and back. I went to her and leaned with my arms on either side of her: she said 'How clever! I will get used to it.' She was still in the shower when the breakfast arrived. I was sitting up in the bed and I called 'Come in.' The waitress was taking lids off plates when Nadia came in with a towel wrapped round her. She said 'How beautiful! I did not know that anything could be so beautiful as this!'

Nadia and I went walking in the hills. We were the same poles of a magnet that would have to fly apart; we were held together by a nuclear force that is stronger than gravity. What a miracle even for a day to be together! Creation has to force what is together apart; but these can still be together at opposite ends of the universe. Sin was the original activity through which grace might abound.

There were sheep grazing on the hills, some with their lambs now almost fully grown. In due course they would be taken to the slaughter and then eaten; what would remain? There would have been humans walking on the hills considering this question.

On the slope there was a fence with strands of wire that seemed to serve no purpose; should it not be common land on the hills?

The sheep watched us as we approached; they showed little interest; they turned away to go on eating. I was holding Nadia by the hand. I thought – What is a sacrament? That of which one partakes to one's salvation or damnation?

A dog had appeared and was chasing the sheep – some large Alsatian. Should we try to stop it? Let it have its way? This was nature. It singled out one sheep and pursued it till the sheep got its head stuck through the wires of the fence; there it remained, presenting its hindquarters to the dog. The dog could now push and pull at it with its teeth as if it were making love. Nadia said 'But it has such thick wool!' I said 'Dogs usually go for the throat.' Nadia said 'Is that why the sheep has got its head through the wire?' I had a memory of the lion cub stretching its teeth round the mouth of the deer; of myself leaning over Nadia. The dog was wrenching at the wool on the sheep's side: the sheep was looking back at it patiently. The dog then lowered its head as if to try to get underneath the sheep: Nadia said 'Perhaps it's hungry.' I thought – You mean the dog might feed not from the sheep's entrails, but from its milk? Nadia took her hand away from mine and approached the dog: the dog bared its teeth at her. She paid no attention to this but knelt at the side of the sheep and felt underneath it. Then she held her other hand out to the dog. I

129

*thought — You mean, the sheep might have lost its lamb and needs
to get rid of its milk? Then — I don't think this will work. The
dog seemed nervous and backed away. Nadia reached between the
dog and the sheep. I thought — But you've done what you can.
Then Nadia seemed to give up; she went to the head of the sheep
and pulled apart the two strands of wire that were trapping it. The
sheep backed clear of the wire. The dog watched it. Nadia said to
the dog 'You've probably already eaten the lamb.' The dog and
the sheep stood still, watching each other. I said 'Perhaps we
should now leave them.' Nadia said 'Yes it might work that way.'
She put her hand in mine again.*

*It seemed important that the day should not last too long or it
might fly out of orbit and disappear. I thought — How does God
stand it! Except that he doesn't, he's shovelled it on to us. So how
can he expect us to know that he exists? Except that he doesn't,
it's up to us. And then it seemed that I had no capacity in my
mind except for exclamations — Nadia, for God's sake Nadia! We
are bearing this! So when we are apart you will not fret about me,
will you, Nadia, and I will not fret about you. The soul gets
blown away but it is one of the bits and pieces of the universe that
cannot stay together because they have to form new galaxies.*

I said 'Nadia, in your religion, do you learn any hymns?'

She said 'We do songs, and dancing.'

'Can you show me?'

*She was wearing a loose-fitting white blouse of thin material
and a soft, patterned skirt that came just below her knees. She
began to dance on the hillside in a controlled yet spontaneous
manner with one arm above her head and the other down her side
as if she were pointing to something beside or just behind her. She
span and strode and checked and became poised; she responded to
the terrain of the hill and made partners of the grass and the slope
— also gravity. They whirled her, let her go, caught her, held her;
they were arms over which she was stretched; they freed her and
she sprang upright like a sapling. She was swept by a wind but*

never went tumbling; she teetered for a moment as if going over and back from a precipice. Towards the end she sang a song that was as soft and gentle as a lullaby. I thought – Lucky galaxies!

When she stopped she said 'Do you know any poems?'

I said 'Yes.'

'Can you tell me one?'

I quoted, occasionally making small gestures with my fingers –

Glory be to God for dappled things –
*   For skies of couple-colour as a brinded cow;*
*   For rose-moles all in stipple upon trout that swim;*
Fresh-firecoal chestnut-falls; finches' wings;
*   Landscape plotted and pieced – fold, fallow, and plough;*
*   And all trades, their gear and tackle and trim.*

All things counter, original, spare, strange;
*   Whatever is fickle, freckled (who knows how?)*
*   With swift, slow; sweet, sour; adazzle, dim;*
He fathers-forth whose beauty is past change:
*   Praise him.*

She said 'Will you be teaching me?'

I said 'No I don't think so.'

'Why not?'

'I learn too much from you.'

'You do?'

'Yes.'

'I am not bad for you?'

'No.'

'I do not know why you are doing these things for me.'

'Yes you do.'

'But not only that.'

'No, but that is how it happens.'

'Yes I see.'

Then when we were walking down the hill to our small hired car, I said 'You become like a sort of god for me.'

'And you have saved me.'

'But now we have to learn things for ourselves.'

'You had to get me here? But have to leave me?'

'I had to learn that from you. Yes.'

It was as if we had lost the instinct for walking. We had to work out the mechanisms of putting one foot in front of the other as if these were the steps of a new dance.

Nadia said 'But Barbara will see me?'

'I hope so.'

'She had no special interest in me?'

'Not at the beginning.'

'She had in you?'

'Perhaps.'

'And that is how things work?'

'It could be.'

'I am frightened.'

'That may be all right.'

'I know that.'

'We will be quiet tonight.'

'You won't go away?'

'No.'

'But tomorrow?'

'I'll take you to the college.'

'I would have liked to know your family.'

'Perhaps you will one day.'

When we got to the car Nadia went round to the far side and she seemed very grown up, no longer a child. We faced each other across the shiny roof of the car and it was as if we were in a buoyant sea. She said 'It will be all right if we can keep our heads above water!' She laughed.

15

After I had been back from America for some time the question that seemed to have broken loose and become a danger to shipping in people's minds was not so much whether it would be right, or had been right, to go to war first with Afghanistan and then with Iraq, as whether the human race had become so confused and duplicitous that there was no point any longer in trying to stop it destroying itself. Military battles could be said to be won; but what was the victory? In Afghanistan there was liberation from oppression but also from restrictions on the burgeoning heroin trade: Iraq was dissolving into guerrilla violence. Where could there be found a passion for the human race to survive? Those who did not wish to partake of terror and anarchy seemed to take refuge in paranoia and silliness. They were kept going by the abundance of things to complain about.

I was rung up by Charlie Richtoven, the man who for years had been, or had been said to have been, Valerie's lover. He said 'Can I come and see you? Are you on your own?'

I said 'My wife Valentina is upstairs.'

'Are your premises bugged?'

'I shouldn't think so. I don't know.'

'Mightn't be a bad thing if they were.'

'Why?'

'The more information the more confusion.'

'You'd like to come now?'

'I'm in a call-box. I didn't know how it works.'

'Come to the downstairs door and knock loudly because I'm rather deaf and the bell doesn't work.'

Before Charlie arrived I tried to remember what Adam told me about him. When young he had inherited a large pharmaceutical company. He was said to have expanded it greatly by involving it in the trade of illegal drugs. He had escaped prosecution, it was hinted, by becoming the supplier of drugs to the American armed forces. It was evident that in some situations soldiers and sailors and airmen acted more expeditiously if obedience was backed by the use of drugs – orders would be carried out without question before or after. This practice was thought to be more economical than the previous conditioning by brutal training: under such routines there had been a growing number of suicides and murders of NCOs and sometimes of soldiers' wives. Under drugs there was an increase of casualties from so-called friendly fire, but this could be passed off as a not unusual feature of war.

When I opened the door to Charlie he was a tall silver-haired man like Henderson but somehow off balance, skew-whiff. He wore dark glasses. I thought – He and Henderson are both in the business of duplicity, tricks. Charlie had with him a large black man whom I took to be a chauffeur or minder. The silver-haired man said 'Shall I tell Charlie to come back in half an hour?' I said 'I thought you were Charlie.' He said 'I am, but for security I'm sometimes Charles.'

He followed me into my room. I thought – He wears dark glasses because he thinks that the black man may be taken as his double? Then – I know this makes no sense.

The man who now called himself Charles said 'I'm trying to get opinions about whether the human race should be wiped out, and what to do if it is found that it should not.'

I said 'And what are you finding?'

'We're entering an age of new fascist totalitarianism. People are locked up indefinitely without trial; it is dangerous to speak one's mind.'

'And that can't just be changed?'

'When God could be a metaphor, it was he who decided. Now we don't believe in metaphors we have lost the power to change; but we have the technology to wipe ourselves out.'

'In that way we can still play God?'

'The weapons have evolved.'

'But God as a metaphor thought there was something worth preserving.'

'Yes, selection makes it more difficult.'

'But evolution's selection.'

'Don't they nowadays call it chance?'

Charlie, or Charles, was going round the room peering at the bits and pieces of folk-art, symbolism, fetishism, that I had collected over the years. I wondered if it was because he had bad eyesight that he wore dark glasses, but this too would make no sense. He said 'What's different now from the time of Noah?'

I said 'I suppose the ugliness.'

'And deception? Self-deception?'

'Oh that's probably the same.'

He came and sat on the sofa that was to one side of my armchair. I thought – Or he wears dark glasses because he wants it to be evident that he knows he is in the dark.

I said 'But we know that human life hangs on threads of innumerable coincidences, so it may not be necessary to use weapons.'

He said 'You mean the dust-cloud that wiped out the dinosaurs may burst any minute from beneath our feet.'

'Or the spread of AIDS. The facilities for masturbation and abortion.'

I tried to remember more of what I had heard about Charlie. He had been reported as saying that all drugs should be freely available so that everybody would have the worthy task of getting off them.

He said 'But extinction is within our control. Preservation may have to be left to chance. You're a gambler?'

'No.'

'But you can see how you can increase the possibilities; spread the uncertainty, the anarchy. Then there's more chance of what's required turning up.'

'But what is required?'

'That will presumably become apparent.'

'You're talking of a practical programme?'

'There are huge losses anyway. You only need one or two winners to survive.'

'You're talking of bluff?'

'I'm talking of science.'

'But the aim could be the opposite of death: change?'

'But you can't talk of aim.'

'No. You can talk of hope. Or you can't really talk at all.'

He had told the black man called Charlie to wait for him. I wondered if this Charlie was standing just outside the door, ready to rush in if there were intimations of lunacy or mayhem.

I said 'So how would you increase the possibilities for change; for survival?'

'You gamble. Risk nonsense. Have fun. Put out a mass of meaningless information or misinformation.'

'About what—'

'Anything. To show the nonsense of things as they are.'

'But that's happening anyway.'

'Yes. Don't you think it's working?'

'Who'd put out the information?'

'Anyone. Everyone. Me. You. You're in a privileged position with your contacts with radio and television.'

He got up from the sofa and went on the prowl again. I tried to imagine him making love with Valerie. They had not had children. He had not thought the odds on their survival favourable.

He said 'Valerie told me to come and see you. I read what you've written.'

'Such as?'

'"Language did not come about to say that we know what things are; it arose to divert us from knowing that we do not."'

'Oh that, yes.'

'So swamp people with information and misinformation, so that they'll know they're in the dark.'

'But what would happen then?'

'That's where luck would come in. Or at least the knowledge that it existed.'

'You mean luck working for one?'

'If that were the case.'

I thought – In some form of existence this conversation is making sense.

But I did not see how I could go on talking with Charlie. It was as if I were having a conversation with a *reductio ad absurdum* of myself. Perhaps this was the point – that I had to stop mocking or trying to explain, and have a conversation with myself. But first I had to move to the sofa and lie down. But Charlie was sitting on it again.

I said 'But you were agreeing that something life-giving might emerge from all this.'

'And you've said that saying that can defeat itself.'

137

'But it can be understood—'

'That's what you're good at saying and not saying: I mean, on the box. People have to say they don't understand you, but they do. The truth as paradox. You get away with it. They go away with it.'

'Yes. No. I see.'

'It only needs a few people. To say it or not say it. To know what's happening.'

'Like that Jewish myth.'

'What—'

'The seven just men who don't know each other and don't themselves know what they are, but who keep the world on course.'

'Oh that, yes. But that you certainly can't say. And I suppose the Jews made the mistake of saying it.'

'But there's no need—'

'No.'

I wondered – Is he Jewish? There's that other myth – of the Wandering Jew who goes round and round the world because he can't accept the idea that it might be God who determines his own limitations, and so becomes a victim.

I said 'But it must be witty.'

'What?'

'The information. Or misinformation—'

'Ah yes!'

'That's what would then be true.'

'Perhaps that's what I came here for.'

I prayed – Will the other Charlie please come soon to pick him up and take him, and indeed perhaps all of us, back to our padded laboratories.

I said 'And what will you be doing about drugs?'

'What?' He seemed to have become slightly distracted, as if he were listening for someone or something beyond the door. He said 'That could be part of an answer.' Then

138

'Though your son Adam doesn't seem to think so.'

'Where is Adam now, do you know?'

'He was working for me for a time. Now he's not.'

'And how's Valerie?'

'She's very fond of you, you know.'

'Yes.'

'They must be witty. Yes. The few just men. I'm most grateful to you for that insight.'

'Oh that's all right.'

'You mean it's state of mind—'

'Like the stuff of the universe.'

'What?'

The large black man called Charlie appeared at the door. He must have been waiting just outside. He was like something emanating from the far side of a mirror. He held out a hand to the other Charlie, who stood up and took it. He said to me 'I may not see you again.'

I said 'Oh I do hope so.'

Then the two Charlies, having become rejoined, went out of the room.

I remained in my chair. Since my return from America it had often been difficult for me to move out of my chair: this had seemed like an operation to separate Siamese twins. I had gone to the Dining Club and to the Hendersons: these had seemed like exercises to give employment to my crutches. Perhaps I had only wanted to move to the sofa because Charlie was sitting on it. But this was the sort of thinking I was trying to let go. I had seen my street accident as in some way destined; but it was not helpful to be taken in too much by one's own myth.

But what was the relationship between consciousness of what happened, and free will?

On and off during my professional life I had tried to propose a theory about how an activity of consciousness might be said to have a physical effect – not on the scale of ordering the universe (though this might be where it would matter) but in something so testable as the activation of a muscle by so-called mind. The theory in fashion was that no such thing as mind existed; so what could be conscious will – in a form, that is, that could be talked about scientifically. A movement of an arm or leg was occasioned by activity of nerves, synapses, genes; the impression that 'one' (whatever 'one' might be) had willed it was an illusion. What happened (this theory held) was that such movement having been occasioned by physical occurrences, part of this activity conveyed the impression to the brain that 'oneself' had willed it; and it was useful for the brain to believe this, because there was an evolutionary advantage in humans imagining that they had free will. But this was not the equivalent of their actually having it (but wasn't it?) even though in comparison with the jargon the idea might seem more 'real'. And so on. But should not more evidence be assembled to see how such things worked? Even if there were no answers, should one not want to see what happened even if their mechanisms were in the dark?

I was sitting in my chair. I said to myself – All right, I will now test these ideas by rising out of this chair and going into the outside world where, all right, some further chance (or not?) events may happen over which I may not have control but which I will have put myself in the way of by getting out of this chair – and so on and so on. But why indeed should any of this be connected to the ordering of the universe? But first, yes – Get up out of this chair!

Nothing happened.

Of course it might have been necessary for my mind, my body, or whatever it was if not me, to teach me, to be taught, a lesson – to show how of course it was possible for nothing to happen. So – so what? I tried again. This time I pushed with my hands so hard that I rose up like a balloon and had to grab the television set in front of me in order to stop myself falling onto my face. I thought – So that is why I've been watching television so assiduously all those weeks! in order that later I would not crash and cause myself further injury. And so on. I straightened as if I were being given a shot of hydrogen or indeed of morphine: I felt so buoyant that I might have to be held back by ropes. I could surely risk going out into the street now with just one crutch: and then I might bowl along like tumbleweed. Of course I would not know where I was going!

When I reached the street it was curiously empty. Was it Sunday? A bank holiday? Another war had begun? Spores of anthrax drifting down like dust.

I was on the pavement beyond our small front garden. I propped myself against the low wall. There I seemed to become immobilised. Had I miscalculated? I should not have ventured out without two crutches? Well what indeed might be the next step in evolution: something to be sure beyond my control.

Approaching along the pavement, keeping close to the walls in front of houses, was a gang of children, ten or twelve years old, trailing their fingers along the tops of the walls or railings as if they were playing a percussion instrument or a harp. A boy was leading them, tapping with a white stick; he did not appear to be blind, but the children following him seemed to be blind or at least partially so; they were feeling and imagining their way with their fingers. I remembered the experiment I had been involved with in the dark: what excitement there had been in discovering one's way rather than taking it for granted! Then I wondered – Or perhaps these children are muggers; the papers are nowadays full of this sort of thing – the flip-over from innocence into savagery. The boy with the white stick had stopped just short of me; it was as if I were blocking his way; but I felt if I left the prop of the wall I would fall over. The boy made strange honking noises like a bird in marshland: I thought – He has lost the faculty of speech; but because he can see he can guide the others who are in other ways defective. They had stopped behind him, bumping into one another gently. I thought – They are like one of those organisms composed of individuals who are not viable on their own, who have formed themselves into a body in order to survive.

There was a girl, slightly bigger than the rest, who stood just behind the boy with her hand on his shoulder. The boy was looking at me, but the girl gazed past me slightly to one side. She said 'Are you all right?' I said 'Yes.' She said 'We are on our way to the zoo, and I wonder if you could tell us how to get there.' I was working out – The boy can see but cannot speak, the girl cannot see but can speak and perhaps can understand the strange noises the boy makes; they must all be from some special school and have been on an outing, and have got lost, or perhaps have broken away. I said 'I can take you to the zoo if you like: that is, if I can get myself off this wall.' She said 'That is very kind of you.' The boy with the stick was making further bird-like noises; he had also taken hold of the girl's hand on his shoulder and seemed to be playing with it, caressing it, giving her messages. The girl said to me 'We can carry you if you like. We can make a chair with our hands, that is one of the things we practise.' I said 'That is extraordinarily kind of you, but once I get going I think I can manage.' The children behind her were coming past her and up to me like shy young animals and were touching me softly as if to find out what I was; then backing away. I said 'Though perhaps it would be useful if you could help me across roads.' The children were murmuring to the girl in a language that I did not understand. The girl laughed: the boy with the stick laughed. I said 'What are they saying?'

The girl said 'They are asking if you're a loony.' Then 'That's what they call grown-ups.' I said 'And what will you tell them?' She spoke to the children. The boy with the stick was helping me to get upright onto my crutch. The girl said 'I've told them that no, I don't think you are a loony.'

16

Adam came to see me, as he had said he would, after I got back from New York. I cannot remember now if this was before or after my meetings with Charlie and with the children. This period of my life seemed to have lost contact with time; as if one of the points of growing old was that things from different periods of one's life might be seen together, reflecting one another, as in some substitute for purgatory.

Adam said 'We were hoping the baby could be born here so that it could have British nationality.'

'So why can't it?'

'Because it's already born.'

'Oh yes of course.'

I did not know if I should express bewilderment about this, play along with it; or if I should or shouldn't show surprise that he was telling me now.

I said 'Then where was it born? What nationality is its mother?'

'That's the problem. The mother still doesn't want to be known as its mother.'

'Why not?'

'She thinks that causes a lot of problems. If you know who

your parents are, you get trapped in their hang-ups that we're all in fact trapped in. And I see that.'

'Oh do you.'

'We've been through this. Nothing personal. It's just a way of trying to alter a state of mind.'

'What state of mind?'

'About ownership. Possession. Caring and feeling cared for, yet letting go free.'

I had not meant to seem to take this personally. Adam should know this. But there were things I wanted to know – also however things probably better left unsaid.

He said 'I mean it's not a programme. It's to be born in mind. The idea is not to have no mother, which is impossible, but to see the possibility of having several mothers, which is not.'

'Not what?'

'Possible or impossible. Then you can choose. Move around.'

'This is mad.'

'Yes. Luckily you can never be sure who your father is, so fathers might be all right.'

I stared at him. He stared back. I thought – Oh well, all right. Then – He's been talking with Charlie? He would want to see the situation as mad?

He said 'I know it's trying to problem-solve and I know that's unfashionable – we're supposed to feel at home with ordinary family miseries.'

'Well they've been tried and tested. Families keep the show on the road.'

'But they don't.'

'Why not?'

'Do you know any decent family that hasn't gone into the ditch and then managed to get out? Do you want the ordinary family show kept on the road?'

'All right. No.' I thought – And we will get used to this?

He said 'I've said I don't think you and Mum were all that bad. But what if you were.'

'You mean if children are brought up in the ordinary straight and narrow, then either they can't rebel or they can't do anything else.'

'So you see, you were good parents.'

'You mean we were so taken up with ourselves that we often hardly knew you were there?'

'But I knew you were there.'

'I see.'

'I could learn what I wanted. I could move around you.'

I thought – That makes us sound like God.

Then – Well if there's nothing for me to do here, I'd better carry on retired.

I said 'All right, so who is the mother?'

'We thought it best if you didn't know.'

'But of course I know!'

'Yes of course you do. I didn't think you wouldn't. The point is for her to feel free about being a mother.'

I thought – How extraordinary that Adam has grown up to be like this! And he is now keeping an eye on us as well as other things—

—Or did God stay on in the Garden as an old-age-pensioner? Not to be too much of a burden on his children?

It is now I am writing this that I am trying to work out when this scene occurred (Why: for clarity? Clarity!) It must have been before Charlie had been to see me because by the time he did Adam had told me about Charlie's pharmaceutical company. But it must also have been after Charlie had come to see me because I remember thinking that the way Adam talked was curiously like that of Charlie – in that he seemed to be making no sense and then suddenly sense was there. So take your pick. Or had he got this from me?

146

(He sometimes said he had.) Or from Valerie? But this scene must surely have taken place after my meeting with Cathy because – because – oh yes, I knew about the baby. And I had had my telephone conversation with my television presenter Tania.

I said to Adam 'But do you still need some help with the authorities?'

'There'll be trouble later if the baby doesn't have some nationality. It'll have my nationality if I adopt it, or any nationality they like, but they say they need to know the mother. Do you think I could say that's sex discrimination?'

'I don't suppose so.'

'I told them it's a curse to have a nationality. Or should be. I don't think they saw this.'

'Can't you say you found it in a dustbin?'

'I tried that. They said – Won't it be unfair on the child when it grows up? I said I thought it would be a fair representation of how a child comes into this world of bureaucracy—'

'But you wanted Valerie and me to seem like responsible grandparents. I'm sorry.'

'Oh well, that might have been just to get you two seeing one another. That worked.'

'Oh I see. Well, what about the story that you found it washed up on a beach like Oedipus?'

'Wasn't that a mountain?'

'Or Moses. Or whatever. So what will you say?'

'Nothing.'

'Nothing?'

'No. I'm going to do what you used to tell me to do, which is giving all considerations an airing, and then see how things work out.'

I thought – You mean, you're confident Cathy will come round.

I was trying to remember an occasion with Adam when he was a child and he had wanted to talk about morals. This was soon after I had moved in with Valentina, and Valerie was in California. (And Adam was still shy with Cathy: this was relevant?) I had gone to say goodnight to Adam on his camp-bed in Valentina's sitting room and he had said – What did happen between you and Mum? She said you were unfaithful on your honeymoon.

– She told you that? When?

– Is it true?

– I don't know.

– What do you mean you don't know?

– It depends on who or what you're being faithful or unfaithful to.

– That's cheating.

– That's life.

Adam had seemed belligerent. I had thought I should say to him – Ask your mother again some time.

Now, some twenty years later, in the basement of the house where I lived with Valentina, I was in my chair and Adam was standing patiently as if he had been waiting to hear what I might be remembering. I thought I might say – I learn as much from you as you from me!

I said 'People do change.'

'Yes. Change what.'

'The way they see the world.'

'Oh that, yes. Well it's best to start with children.'

'But it would be the same old people who were starting with children—'

'Look. Women both want to be and don't want to be mothers. So they screw things up. They take it out on the children.'

'And fathers don't even begin.'

'But they might if mothers didn't feel so resentful.'

I was trying to remember when Adam had stopped being shy of Cathy. This was a timing indeed impossible to pin down. I said 'But when I talked to you about that sort of stuff – I mean people changing the way they see things – that was when you were – what – thirteen, fourteen? Did I talk to Cathy?'

'She used to listen.'

'But she always had her own ideas.'

'Yes. But perhaps she also wanted not to feel so much alone.'

'But has that got something to do with – what – why she doesn't want to be known as the mother of the baby now?'

'I don't know if she wants to be or not. She's recently seen too much of this shitty world. She wanted to do something about it but directly, yes.'

'And having done that she now might want to be a mother?'

'Which is more difficult because there are such paradoxical injunctions—'

'Oh those, yes—'

'—to be responsible and to let go free—'

'And that's what you're waiting for? To become like God?'

I was beginning to feel exhausted. I was thinking – But there is something being worked out, and of course it's in the dark, and of course it's exhausting.

Adam said 'Do you remember that time when I asked you if you'd been unfaithful to my mother on your honeymoon, and you said I should ask her again?'

'Yes.'

'Well I did.'

'And what did she say?'

'She said she didn't know.' Adam laughed.

I thought – Well that's all right.

I said 'But who else have you got looking after the baby?'

He said 'Well there's a friend of Cathy's looking after it now.'

'She is?'

'Yes. But could I bring it round to you for a couple of days when I haven't got anyone else?'

'You'd like to do that?'

'Yes.'

'Valentina would have to know.'

'Can't you say it's yours?' Then 'That was a joke!'

'But why don't you want Valentina to know? I haven't understood that yet.'

'Cathy's very protective of Valentina. She doesn't want Valentina to feel inadequate. But she might be doing just that. You could help her get on with things.'

I thought – Who: Cathy? Valentina?

Then – That's why you'd bring the baby round here?

I said 'Yes. Valentina learns.'

Adam said 'And you were very fond of Cathy.'

I was being overwhelmed by sleep as was happening to me with ever more farcical frequency. And then I dreamed. But I hardly ever remembered my dreams. Things went on in that mysterious world while things were being left to work themselves out off (or was it on?) stage.

When I woke up Adam had gone. Well what had been worked out? How would I know.

I thought I might try to get hold again of Tania, my television presenter. Was there some connection, between Tania and Nadia? Or did I mean Tania and Cathy? But I had got through to Tania not so long ago and she had said, yes, that she was in Jerusalem with the baby.

That could have been a joke? A metaphor?

But a friend of Cathy's was now looking after the baby?

Perhaps I should go on with my story of the two people on the shore of the Dead Sea. Had they turned turtle yet? Had they tried floating the baby? Does turning turtle mean going onto your front or onto your back?

Perhaps I should get hold of Cathy. But I had nothing to say.

Perhaps I should do nothing.

I heard Valentina arriving home. She did not go upstairs first to deposit coat, bag, parcels, as she usually did, but came in at the basement door looking like Aquarius the water-carrier.

She said 'You knew!'

'I knew what?'

'I thought they didn't want me to tell you.'

'I thought they didn't want me to tell you!'

'But why?'

'I don't know. Perhaps they wanted us to come together in an embrace in the face of their dottiness.'

I thought – Cathy told you? Then she'll definitely come round!

Valentina said 'I suppose I'd have been so bossy.'

'And you'd have thought it was all your fault. And I'd have thought it was an interesting problem.'

'So they were right not to tell us? But of course we knew all the time!'

'Yes.'

'I suppose you think it's all right for a child not to know who its parents are—'

'Well of course it can know. Or not, if it likes.'

'But are you saying that none of this has really been the point? The point has been to get Cathy round to seeing the point of being a mother?'

'To see the possibility—'

'And to get us both to be concerned and understand and not interfere—'

'—in this terrible world where people's instincts are to gobble up everyone including their children—'

'You think it will work out?'

'I don't know.'

'I still think Adam wants a harem of mothers for his children.'

'Possibly.'

I thought suddenly – Might Nadia have had a baby? Surely I would have known!

Then – No, how would I have known, if that had not been in the way it was working out.

17

When the blind or partially blind children had bumped into me in the street and had inquired – Was I a loony? – this had stirred my memory of my time with Nadia and the question that had haunted me afterwards – well was I a loony, not so much for what I had done or said, but for letting her go. This had seemed at the time to be natural and inevitable: but why? It was as if the answer to this lay over the horizon of the beautiful hills where we had walked. But when had my feelings or dealings with Nadia ever made sense? From the beginning they had seemed to occur in a world which had different values and made different demands; the style of which was not the customary one of the need to keep things going, but of crisis, risk, the need for change. Then there was the actual world again: but what was the point of so alarmingly winning what I was going to give up?

When the children had bumped into me and there was the speculation about whether I should be called a loony this was accompanied by such laughter that the children had to hang on to each other as if to stop themselves being blown away. The boy with the white stick made such strange noises that the girl with her hand on his shoulder tugged his ear as if to get him to stop; our area of pavement became the scene of all manner of embraces. The streets were usually frequented by people who used their faculty of sight to steer clear of bumping into one another let alone embracing; there was a couple even now crossing the road in order to avoid us. I was thinking – To them we will appear loonies.

We set off along the pavement with my one crutch making me lopsided like a boat in a high wind, the girl and the boy on the other side to balance me, the rest of the children strung out behind like the tail of a kite. There were a number of crossings to be negotiated before we reached the park beyond which there was the zoo: I worried that our ungainly crocodile might get mown down by traffic. I had felt before that I should perhaps take up the children's offer to carry me because this would make them feel useful: also then as a tight-knit group it would be easier for traffic to spot us – or if not, at least we might all become extinct at once. By the time we came to the first major crossing four of the boys were in fact already practising making a seat for me with interlocking hands and wrists: what image could they have of me – if not a loony, then a child? The others were jostling to give advice. I wondered suddenly – Might these children in some real or imagined world be the orphaned children I had helped rescue from Kosovo? Their ages did not make this impossible. Then when I put my arms round the shoulders of two of the boys who were making a seat for me my crutch flailed outwards and became a menace to other people waiting at the lights. The boy made his bird-like noises and the girl was talking in their strange language, and I thought I'd better set off on my own across the road. I got halfway and I held my arms out to stop the traffic or to seem to invite immolation. Traffic stopped. I thought – Some gestures are effective in real or imaginary worlds.

When we reached the park one or two of the children ran

free and held their arms out and banked and swooped like aeroplanes. They knew how to do this? The rest of us moved in a tight-knit group like a VIP protected by bodyguards; the girl walked beside me and I put my hand on her shoulder. She said 'Do you often come to the zoo?' I said 'I used to.' She said 'What did you come here for?' I said 'I like watching the animals and wondering what goes on in their minds.'

'And what do you think does?'

'I don't know, probably quite like us, but they're better at accepting things.'

'But aren't they in cages?'

'Yes, but in the wild they're always eating or being eaten.'

The boy with the white stick broke away and ran ahead and did a whirling dance on the grass. The girl said 'We were planning to try to let the animals out, even if we were eaten.'

I thought of saying – But in the wild things don't seem much to mind being eaten. I had a vision of the animals and the children playing a game as if of hide-and-seek.

We had to go out onto the pavement again for the short walk to the zoo entrance. The boy got the children together by a series of calls and whistles. I said 'Now it's just a short walk to the zoo but you must stay close together and be quiet or they may not let you in.' The girl said 'Why might they not let us in?' I said 'They might think that you would get yourselves eaten.' The children became quiet.

At the turnstile there was a man in a box with a glass front with a small opening at the bottom through which, when he became aware of us, he seemed to be trying to put his head as if it were a guillotine. He said 'Are you in charge of these children?' I said 'Yes.' I thought of saying – There's no one in charge, we're an example of a symbiotic organism having come about in the course of evolution. The man was getting his head back through the hole in the glass: he said 'I need you to sign this form absolving the management from responsibility.' I shouted 'Oi!' The boy had been rattling his stick against the bars of the turnstile and the children were climbing and squeezing over, under, through. I said to the man 'You'd better let me through or you'll be responsible!' I still had my hand on the shoulder of the girl. The man in the box worked a mechanism and we went through. The girl said 'I think we make people feel guilty.'

The children had at first scattered when they got through the gate; now they were coming together again like fishes. I had given no thought to what to do when we got into the zoo: I had seen my task as just to get the children there. It might have been possible to take them round the cages and give them a short lecture on the animals in each, but I did not think they would want this. I remembered a Sufi saying – It is sometimes a blessing to abandon people.

I said to the girl 'Can you tell them to follow us to the café, where I'll get a table, and then they'll know where to come back to when they go off again.' The boy with the stick came up and the girl said something to him in their language and he went after the children and got them formed up in a gang again. There was a space in front of the café with tables and chairs. I remembered – I used to come here with Adam when he was little and there was the treat of riding on an elephant. I sat at a table and said to the girl 'Tell them there will be cakes and Coca-Colas and ices waiting for them here. Otherwise they can explore.' The girl spoke to them and they eddied round the table and chairs as if to memorise them; then wandered off slowly taking care to keep together. I thought – When they are on their own they are like people who are simply fond of one another. They were heading towards the terraces where there were antelope? deer? – I could not remember – but also bears and wolves? With a deep drop into a chasm which was supposed to separate the animals from humans, but into which indeed these children might fall. And then I would be responsible.

A waitress had come up to take my order. She reminded me of someone, I could not remember who. The children had veered off and were now running and bumping round an enclosure that might contain – otters? beavers? I remembered the fun of hide-and-seek in the dark. The waitress said 'What are they, blind?' I said 'Yes.' She said 'How do they see when they're blind?' I said 'I think some of them must be able to see something.' She was a young dark-haired girl with delicate features: I thought – Perhaps it is just that she reminds me of a dancer. She said 'Are you in charge of them?' I said 'Not really, I just said that I'd get them here.' She said 'They seem happy.'

An elephant had come into view at the far end of the wide open space in front of the café. The elephant was carrying people, mostly children, on a contraption on its back; it was being led by a young keeper with long fair hair, dressed in white overalls. The boy with the stick and the girl with her hand on his shoulder had separated themselves from the others and were approaching the place where there was a mounting-block for people to climb onto or down from the elephant's back. The elephant came to this place and stopped. The girl and the boy stood by the elephant's head; the boy was pointing with his stick and seemed to be describing the elephant to the girl with his strange noises.

People were climbing down from the elephant; there was a small queue of people waiting to climb up. The waitress I had been talking to left my table and went to the keeper in white overalls and said something to him; then she turned and spoke to the people in the queue. The elephant raised its trunk and emitted a mournful bellow: the boy by the elephant's head jumped up and down excitedly. The rest of the children were congregating at the bottom of the steps: the people had finished climbing down but the people in the queue were not yet climbing up, because the elephant seemed to be restless. The waitress gave the keeper a quick kiss on the cheek and then went to where the children were waiting and took two of them by the hand and led them to the steps. The others followed, except the boy and the girl, who stayed by the elephant's head. Some of the people who had been queuing were now helping the children up the steps: I thought – This is an operation of grace.

The girl with the boy had put a hand out and was feeling the elephant's trunk: then she put both arms round the trunk and hugged it. I thought – What was the name of that horse that pulled a chariot up to the sun? The boy seemed to be talking to the elephant; the elephant was making a faint wheezing sound. The keeper was at the top of the steps seeing the children into the howdah on the elephant's back. I thought – Of course it has made a difference that the waitress is pretty.

I became aware of a disturbance going on in the direction of the zoo entrance. I thought – Oh well, it may be the people who were in charge of the children when their bus overturned or they had gone shopping or whatever; they have now come to reclaim the children; they would have known where they would be heading. The elephant had lowered the end of its trunk almost to the ground and the girl was now seating herself on it astride – holding on with her hands and knees as if on a pony's back. I thought – Let there just be time for them to have their ride to the sun. The boy was dancing in front of the elephant waving his stick as if he were a musical conductor; or one of those bees that tell other bees where there is honey. I left the café table and joined the waitress who had by now, with the help of the keeper and some of the people who had been queuing, got all the children up and safely strapped into the seats on the elephant's back. I said to the waitress 'Are you a dancer?' She said 'Yes, I do ballet.' I said 'Where?' She said 'I hope Covent Garden.' I said 'I'll come and see you sometime.'

There was a posse of people running from the direction of the entrance. The elephant set off at a lumbering trot with the boy with the stick prancing in front of it and the girl hanging on to its trunk which it now lifted high into the air and the children on its back waving and laughing. The keeper at the bottom of the steps became surrounded by people gesticulating and exclaiming: he was paying no attention to them: he was watching the children on their way to the sun. The waitress said 'I'll make it up to him if he gets the sack.' The keeper put his fingers in his mouth and emitted a piercing whistle.

The elephant was going past a monkey house and I had a vision of the monkeys at last having something to interest them in their otherwise boring lives. With luck the elephant-chariot might reach the lions and tigers who after millions of years might at last learn to smile. I said to the waitress 'I've left some money on the table for the Coca-Colas and cakes and ices.' She said 'Aren't you staying?' I said 'No, I think we've done enough.' She said 'Well come and see me dance in three years' time.' The people who had been queuing were talking to the people who had come running; everyone seemed to be calming down; I had begun to feel as if I might fall over. The elephant came into sight again, walking, with the boy with the stick now turning occasional cartwheels at its tail. The elephant came back to the steps. There was a moment when no one seemed to know what to do: then the children were being helped down, and the waitress was talking to the people who had come from the entrance, and the elephant lowered its trunk close to the ground and the girl who was sitting astride it was getting off. The waitress was pointing to the café and the children and the people who had come for them were moving tentatively towards it. The boy with the stick held out his hand to the girl and she seemed to see where to take it; he helped her down. I thought – This whole thing has been a ballet. The boy and the girl stood side by side and now he was pointing with his stick in my direction and the girl seemed to see me and smiled. I thought – I may never be able to get home on my own with just one crutch: but never mind, in a ballet there can be miracles.

18

When I had felt it impossible to set off on my own from the zoo across the park – having been supported on my way there by the girl as well as my having the task of showing the children the way – what had happened then? I could not with certainty remember. I had felt dizzy, there was too much going on in my mind, I felt as if I were having a stroke. I was the first of my species in a strange environment; all the animals, humans, even the children, had their cages or niches; how should I be expected to survive? Would it not be best if I collapsed and was carried off somewhere, anywhere, by paramedics—

—Or were there bulrushes in which I could hide?

But then there I was, apparently lurching lopsided along the pavement. Had there been enough in my mind for me to have confidence in what might be going on apart from it? Dancers give an impression of things being ordered beyond the confines of their bodies. In crossing a road I would be like tumbleweed; yes, blown by a wind.

This we had to get accustomed to?

When I arrived home on my one leg and one crutch I began to tell Valentina the story of the children rather than of my hazardous journey home, but this too sounded so unlikely that I found myself saying 'I don't suppose I'm getting all the details right.' Valentina said 'No I don't suppose you are.' Then 'Well if you can spend an afternoon with children at the zoo, perhaps you can come out a bit more with me.'

I said 'But you don't want me to come out with you.'

'I've just said that I do.'

I thought – Well things do change.

The occasion that arose to which Valentina said she would like me to accompany her was a party for the launch of a book by a fashionable interior decorator. It struck me that this might not be so different from a trip to the zoo, though it seemed not worth working out why. I was no longer seeing myself as a clown-like figure having to rail against the absurdities of the contemporary world: why shouldn't people enjoy, while they could, the confines of their zoo.

The party for the interior decorator was being held in a shop. Well yes, it would make sense to think that anything in the world of art and fashion should now be exhibited in a shop; people were entertained and kept going at least by money. On display in fact were some rather beautiful objects – glass and china like rocks and shells at the bottom of the sea; fabrics like waterfalls of gold and silver sand. It was the people who were strangely drab, like squids or fish with huge eyes under great pressure. I said to Valentina 'I thought these people were supposed to be beautiful.' She said 'They are if you have an eye.' I thought – An eye for the struggles of people trying to make themselves beautiful? Perhaps they need to be photographed. Valentina said 'Perhaps we should find you somewhere to sit down.'

I looked for a chair, but chairs had cords stretched across them to keep them in condition for sale. I thought – I have been too long away from highways and byways to be used to what appearances are like.

In my search for somewhere to sit I drifted from Valentina: I found myself in an unfrequented part of the shop where there were items of garden furniture. There was a swing-sofa which reminded me of the one on which years ago I had sat with Barbara on our verandah waiting for Nadia to pass by. I had never inquired further into why Barbara had become so willing to help me with Nadia, because it had seemed that this might be tempting fortune. I thought I might now sit on the sofa as if to test it for bounce and resilience; perhaps to swing back to ghosts of the past for a while. Might I then see these with a less haunted eye? I might even stretch out on the sofa and have a quick sleep while appearing to be testing it for size. Or to the fashionable world it might seem that I was an advertising gimmick.

I stepped over a low cord and sat on the swing-sofa. It bounced. Perhaps I would turn turtle and find out what I wanted about the Dead Sea. Would I be looking at the sky, or the landscape on the bottom.

Barbara had been very good to me and Nadia. Nadia had told me that I should be good to Barbara, and I had never really done this, being confused and wanting to put things out of mind. But now, swinging gently, I might be lulled into some sort of confidence. Might I even try to get through to Barbara on my mobile phone?

Barbara had made the practical arrangements for Nadia to come to England – for her acceptance by the university; for the necessary grants or bursary or whatever. I had provided the necessary recommendation. Barbara had joked that she might be doing this to get revenge on me; but this had been a joke? I had imagined that Barbara must be fond of me. But none of this now seemed the point. What had been happening to Nadia?

I would have to get Barbara's number from directory inquiries. There were now new numbers for getting in touch with inquiries: how does one inquire about these. I said 'Hullo? Hullo?' The comments being conveyed to me made no sense. I had read somewhere that the people running the new inquiry system often deliberately made no sense in order to earn more money. This seemed not unlikely.

Valentina approached. She said 'What on earth are you doing?' I said 'I thought it would look as if I was trying out this sofa for bounce and size.'

'Have you been asleep?'

'I don't think so.'

'There's nothing wrong with the people at this party.'

'I've realised that. I thought I should try to get through to Barbara on my mobile phone to put things right. You remember Barbara? Barbara Gifford. She was with me at Oxford, and then in Iran.'

'No I don't remember Barbara.'

'We used to sit on a swing-sofa like this.'

'Oh really. Here, let me—'

'I want to thank her, but I don't know her number. And now the inquiries people make more money by giving you wrong information rather than right. Have you heard about this? Or it might be one of Charlie von Richtoven's promotions.'

'Where was she at Oxford?' Valentina had taken the telephone.

'Oriel. She was a don. But that was years ago.'

'They should have a number.'

I was thinking – I can't imagine why everyone is being so nice to me: perhaps it is because I have been knocked on the head. Or perhaps Valentina has worked out that if it were not for Barbara and indeed Nadia, I would not be with her now. And she thinks this is all right?

Or is Valentina just someone who (thank heavens) likes to be in control?

I had just once taken Barbara out to dinner after I had been with Nadia. She had said – You don't have to. I had said – Oh I think I do! We had gone to a smart restaurant where I had drunk a lot of wine and Barbara had said – Well it's done now, we'll see what happens. I had thought – Oh yes, the jolly old what-happens.

Valentina was holding the telephone out to me. As I reached for it the sofa lurched and almost deposited me upside down on the floor. (Had I been asleep? Dreaming of the Dead Sea?) Valentina said 'Here, for God's sake, I don't want to go through all that again.'

I said 'What—'

'Barbara.'

'You've got Barbara? How do you do such things!'

I took the telephone. Valentina moved away. I thought – But things don't just happen, no. You have to work at something or other.

I said 'Barbara?'

Barbara's voice said 'It's a good thing I can talk to you.'

'Yes I've been trying to get through to you.'

'So your wife says. I suppose it's what you call synchronicity.'

'Yes.'

'Can you meet me?'

'I'm at a party at a shop in Sloane Street.'

'I know. I'll meet you at that hotel in Sloane Square in fifteen minutes.'

'I'm a bit immobile.'

'So your wife told me. Your new wife.'

'Yes.'

'You always used to say "I see."'

'Yes.' Barbara rang off. I had been going to say – All right, I'll meet you in fifteen minutes – but perhaps this hadn't been necessary.

I pushed myself off the swing-sofa which recoiled and hit me at the back of the knees but I was ready for this, I had been thinking I might fall and flop about like a footballer. I made my way to the door of the shop: I was walking with two sticks: I wondered – Do I want to be thought more or less lame than I am? I peered into the street. It was only two hundred yards to the square: the hotel which Barbara had alluded to was presumably the one to which I had taken her for dinner years ago. So she remembered that, did she? But why had she never afterwards tried to get in touch with me?

I set off briskly. I had got about halfway to the square when a car drew up beside me and the passenger door opened and a voice said 'Get in.'

I said 'Whoa! Help!'

Barbara said 'Give me your sticks.'

I said 'Someone did mug me in New York.'

Barbara said 'I know. Do you know who?'

'No.'

'You might have been lucky. But then you always were.'

When I had managed to fit myself into Barbara's small car she set off, and then went past the hotel and round the square. She said 'There's something I've been meaning to tell you.'

I said 'Yes I've been wanting to talk to you too.'

'Do you know why Nadia had to get out of Iran? Why her family wanted her out?'

I said 'To further her education.'

'No. Not just that. She'd killed someone.'

'Killed someone.'

'Yes. Someone who was trying to rape her. When she was still almost a child. Twelve, thirteen. At least that's what I was told.'

'I see.'

'It was hushed up. Which it was obviously in everyone's

interests to do. Someone from a neighbouring family. Do you see?'

'I suppose so.'

I thought – Well I never really supposed they all saw me as the Archangel Gabriel.

Barbara said 'Once she was grown up, then the other family might think it was their duty to take revenge. That's how it works. Family honour, dishonour, and so on.'

'How did she kill him?'

'With a knife.'

'You don't think it's just a story?'

'What?'

I went on quickly 'And had he managed to rape her?'

'That's what I thought I'd have to ask you.'

'No I don't think so. But it's so unlikely!'

'Of course it's not just a story. What would have been the point.'

'To get her to further education.'

'Oh I see.'

We were driving round Sloane Square for the second or third time. We were both staring ahead intently as if at difficult traffic.

Barbara said 'The old women of the village knew. They enrolled me. They have their own brand of feminism.'

'They wanted you to get Nadia out?'

'They knew I'd be sympathetic. We'd talked about such things. They saw that you might be useful.'

'You could have done it on your own.'

'Perhaps I hadn't got the guts.'

'You could always blame me?'

'I did warn you!'

'But why didn't you tell me—'

'You might not have done it.'

'Of course I would have done it!'

167

'Well, I couldn't know. And then it seemed too late to tell you.'

We were still grinding round the square. I thought – If we go on long enough some actual walls may fall down.

Barbara said 'But the point is, with all these asylum-seekers, fundamentalists, potential terrorists, coming over now, she might be in danger again. And so might you. There are said to be people making inquiries. That's what I thought when I heard you'd been hit in New York.'

'Oh I was making jokes!'

'How do you know? I did have to give assurances that Nadia was a seeker of asylum from danger.'

'Then at least that was true.'

I was thinking – There's something magical, potent, is there not, about a young girl who kills for honour or whatever you call it. Judith, Deborah—

Barbara said 'I'm afraid this must be a shock for you.'

I said 'No, it's wonderful, it explains everything. Makes it natural, not miraculous. Or is that truly miraculous? A blessing.'

'Why?'

'There was always something not quite proper about just lust!'

'Which it was.'

'It didn't feel like that, no.'

'I shall never understand you. I thought you'd be angry that I deceived you.'

'Oh well, who cares. Look how it turned out!'

'I might have been destroying your marriage.'

'Oh no. It was given a push.'

'It needed that?'

'Well here we are.'

I was thinking – And now I should be able to see Nadia again!

I said 'What has Nadia been doing all these years?'

Barbara had been driving slower and slower round the square. It seemed that she might be about to cease. She said 'She got her degree. She went on to study comparative religion.'

'Where?'

'Here and there.'

'Are you in touch with her?'

'I could be.'

'Will you tell her that you've told me?'

'You won't take it out on her?'

'Good God no! Don't you see? Something that might have been manipulative, self-serving, has been all the time—' I groped for a word that did not seem to exist.

I thought – I'd better be getting back to the party.

Barbara said 'I think I'd better drop you back at the party.'

I was checking through words as if in a thesaurus – pragmatic? holy?

When I did get back to the party – many people still not drinking much except water because they were alcoholics – I could not at first find Valentina; so I went back to the swing-seat and sat with my hands behind my head and said – Nadia, Nadia, I am so terribly grateful! for trusting me, for trusting us, for trusting that everything is for the best in the best of all possible worlds. And we did glimpse this? When we had come down from the hills and were looking at each other across the roof of the car and had thought – We will not drown!

I saw Valentina standing over me. I said 'I just popped out to see Barbara.' She said 'Yes I know.' I said 'How?' Valentina said 'She came back for a moment after she'd dropped you because she'd forgotten to tell you something.' I said 'What?' Valentina said 'That she doesn't know Nadia's address, but she'll manage to get a message through to her, so that if she wants to get in touch with you, she can.' I said 'Oh thank you Valentina!' Valentina said 'What for?' I said 'For being so good to me, darling Valentina!'

19

Adam rang me to tell me that Valerie was ill in California. Since this was serious enough for him to have telephoned, I wondered if she might be dying. I said 'Is Charlie looking after her?' Adam said 'I don't think they're together.'

'Could you possibly go out and see her? I don't think I'd make it.'

'Yes, that's why I'm ringing. Could you possibly have your go at looking after the baby?'

'Yes of course. I'll tell Valentina.'

'No don't.'

'But Valentina knows about the baby!'

'Yes I know, but it's still a bit complicated.'

'You want to bring it round here?'

'Yes please. I've got a girl who helps with it, but she's away for a couple of days. She'll be back to pick it up from you tomorrow.'

'You want to bring it now?'

'I'm afraid it's an awful imposition.'

'As a matter of fact Valentina is away for a couple of days too. Did I tell you?'

'Yes I think you did as a matter of fact.'

I thought – So it's not all that complicated.

I said 'I'll manage fine.'

'It's very good of you.'

'No, it'll keep my mind off things.'

'Perhaps that's what babies are for.'

What I wanted my mind to be kept off was my impatience to see Nadia again. This was after Barbara had told me that she would tell Nadia she could get in touch with me. Why had Barbara not told me her address? Because she was not sure that Nadia would want to see me? But what was I hoping – that we could go back to a fork in the road at the end of the day when we had gone walking in the hills? No, not that. Then what? These were questions in my mind like a dog barking.

Adam was saying 'I'll bring her round now.'

'Oh it's a her is it?'

'Yes, didn't I tell you?'

I was thinking – Perhaps the girl who'll come to pick the baby up tomorrow will be a Scandinavian au pair.

When Adam had rung off I tried to turn my mind to what it should be concerned about, which was Valerie's illness. I could have questioned Adam more about this; but I had become so taken over recently by the idea of events occurring for a purpose rather than being occasioned by a cause, that there was not much sensibly to worry about because the future could not be foretold. One might however turn to the past for suggestions.

There had been a time soon after I had moved in with Valentina when she and I had gone on a holiday to Rome, driving down through France and northern Italy. Then when we reached Rome there was a message from Adam saying that Valerie had returned unexpectedly to London from America because she was ill, and would I ring him. I was still married to Valerie at this time, and the future of Valentina and myself was naturally uncertain. In Rome I told Valentina of the message and she said 'And I suppose now you'll go back.' I said 'I'll speak to Adam.' Valentina said 'Will you always go back every time she summons you?' I said 'That's not her sort of trick.'

'Then what is?'

'If I do go back, just for a day, I could sort out everything with her.'

Cathy was spending the two weeks we were away with her father, and Valentina had been understandably anxious about this. So I said 'Also, I could see that Cathy is all right.' Valentina said 'Ah, that's your sort of trick!'

So I rang Adam, and he said that Valerie had come back to London because she had to have an operation to remove a cyst from her inside. When Adam had told her I was in Italy she had made him promise not to tell me because she said she did not want to spoil my holiday. I said to Adam 'But of course I'll come back, at least for a day. That is, if you think she'd like that.' He said 'Yes I think she'd like that.' I said 'Don't let them operate till I get there.'

Valentina had been listening. She said 'Does she even know you're with me?' I said 'I'm sure Adam will have told her.'

'She hasn't been near you for six months!'

'No, but this is her way of doing things.'

I wondered if Valentina would say she would fly back with me to London, in which case I did not think that things would sort themselves out. As I was packing an overnight bag she said 'Aren't you afraid of what I'll get up to when I'm left alone in Rome?' I said 'Yes, but you've always said you wanted to see Rome.' She said 'I don't believe you have ordinary feelings about anything.' I said 'No I don't think ordinary feelings are interesting.' She said 'Then what is?' I thought of saying – Right and wrong; but I did not think one could say this. I said 'What happens.'

I was recalling this years later while I was waiting for Adam to turn up with his baby. There was also that other bit of conversation I used to have with Adam — You can't change the world but you can change the way people see the world.

When Adam arrived the baby was asleep in a portable cot and was hardly visible within blankets. It seemed quite a large baby. I wondered if I should pick it up and make cooing noises, but I did not think Adam would be impressed by this.

I said 'It looks so trusting.'

Adam said 'It sort of grows on you.'

I thought — We both go on referring to it as 'it'.

I said 'Do you remember that time years ago when Valerie got ill and I was with Valentina in Rome and you were at school and you left a message and I flew back?'

He said 'Yes, I think that was one of the things that made me see things differently.'

'It did?'

'Before that I'd been apt to see us as a dysfunctional family. After that I didn't.'

'Good heavens!'

'Haven't I told you that?'

'No. I've been thinking about that time.'

'I thought we were not conventional nor moral, but functional.'

'About one another? About bringing up children?'

'Look, I'd better catch my plane.'

I thought — Yes one shouldn't push one's good fortune too far.

He took a plastic bag from the end of the carry-cot and said 'Here's food, bottle, nappies. And various unguents, or whatever, with instructions.'

I said 'And a beautiful Swedish au pair will be arriving in the morning.'

He said 'Oh yes, a beautiful au pair may be arriving any minute!' Then he hurried away.

I thought – Oh well, what does that mean? Yes I see. Do I?

I sat in my chair and thought that if I kept just enough of an eye on the baby but not too much, then it might feel at ease and not wake up. I tried to go back to the time when Valerie had previously been ill and I had flown back from Rome.

I had worried that Valerie might already have had the operation before I had been able to give my opinion about it, which for some reason I thought she was requiring me to do. Was this functional? I was not worrying so much about whether Valentina would get herself picked up in Rome, because the effects of this should be remediable whereas getting oneself cut up might not be.

Yes, this was functional.

When I reached the hospital I went to the ward and found the sister and said 'Have they done the operation yet?' She said 'No, she's waiting for someone to sign the dispensation.' I said 'That might be me.' Valerie was in a private room and was sitting up in bed looking pale and fierce. She said 'I told Adam not to ring you.' I said 'Yes, so he told me.' She said 'Were you having a nice time?' I said 'Quite, thank you.' She said 'I've got a cyst in my inside and they've got to take it out but at the same time they want to do a hysterectomy.' I said 'Why?' She said 'The doctor calls it killing two birds with one stone, which I thought was quite witty.' I said 'Yes, but not much of a reason to have a hysterectomy.' She said 'Oh I am glad you've come!' I said 'Oh that's all right.'

A doctor and a staff nurse came and we discussed the advantages and disadvantages of someone of Valerie's age having a hysterectomy. The doctor said 'You'll probably have to have it done sometime anyway.' Valerie said 'Why, how old am I?' The nurse said 'You're nearly fifty.' Valerie said 'I thought I was in my forties.' The doctor said 'But that means you shouldn't have any more babies.' Valerie said 'I thought my cyst might be an ectopic pregnancy.' I said 'What's that?' The doctor said 'A bit of a non sequitur.' I thought – Well that's witty too. Valerie said to me 'I should have told you that Charlie Richtoven's here.' I said 'Oh is he?' Then I began to worry about Valentina in Rome: I should not be too long in getting back. The doctor said 'Does that mean that you don't want a hysterectomy?' Valerie said 'Yes, I mean no, I don't think I do.' She said to me 'Is that right?'

So Valerie had her cyst removed but not her womb; and I stayed in London for two or three days and visited her. I tried to telephone Valentina but the hotel always said that she was out. I went for long walks again and it seemed that we all had to be on our own for a time to be responsible for what would happen next – for the break-up and reforming of relationships. Adam met me in the hospital and said 'Did I do the right thing to ring you?' I said 'Yes.' He said 'Did Valentina come back with you?' I said 'No, she stayed in Rome.'

'Mum was anxious that she might have mucked up you and Valentina.'

'No, that's all right.'

'You know she had a row with Charlie, I think it was about her wanting to ask you about the operation.'

'But she told you not to ring me.'

'Yes, but I think Charlie thought that was for his benefit.'

I tried to work this out. I said 'But you mean you think they're all right now?' Adam said 'Yes I think they'll sort it out.'

I once saw a man who I thought must be Charlie lurking behind some metalwork in the huge central atrium of the hospital. When he saw me he did not try to duck out of sight but stood quite still. I wondered – He recognises himself as part of these relationships that are functional and work themselves out?

Before I left to go back to Rome I asked Adam if he'd seen anything of Cathy. He said 'Yes, her father seems a bit wacko, but I think she's got him where she wants him.'

When I got back to Rome I said to Valentina 'Did you have a nice time?' She said 'Yes, I saw the Vatican and the Colosseum and St Peter's, and a church outside the walls which I bet you'll say you know.' I said 'No, never heard of it.'

I was recalling this after Adam had brought his baby round to me before he went to fly out to see Valerie in California. These two occasions of Valerie being ill became entwined in my mind, with the image of Valerie's choosing not to have a hysterectomy connecting to the presence of this baby. It was still sleeping. I wondered – Is there some significance in our going on calling it 'it' rather than 'her'? I watched some television news with the sound turned off: there was a slapstick metaphysical argument still going on about the existence or non-existence of weapons of mass destruction. In some alternative universe this would surely be seen as funny?

I peered in at the baby every now and then; it seemed both defenceless and resolute. I thought – Well you'd better try to be functional: your mother says she doesn't want you crucified.

I became aware of someone moving quietly on the floor above my basement. There should be no one else in the house; or had Valentina come back from Rome with a lover? No, that was in another memory-warp: Valentina was in Denmark giving a seminar on ordinary human hang-ups. Was it this that had put into my head the idea of a Scandinavian au pair? Had Nadia really killed someone who was trying to rape her when she was twelve, thirteen? But there was definitely someone coming down the stairs to my room, treading quietly.

I sat with my arms rigidly along the sides of my chair. Might it be a relief, the idea that someone might want to do away with me and kidnap the baby? The door into my room began to open slowly. There had been too many horror films for this to be frightening; nowadays one just wondered what sort of monster the make-up people would come up with. A head appeared round the door. It was Cathy's. I said 'I knew it was you!' She said 'Oh of course you didn't!' I said 'I just didn't want to put it into words in case this stopped it happening.' She went to the table on which Adam had left the carry-cot and peered down into it cautiously. I said 'Well it had to be someone who both had a key to the house and wanted to have a look at the baby.' Cathy said 'Everyone wants to have a look at babies.' She was picking it up and holding it with her cheek against its head. I thought – In pictures of the Virgin she does not often do this: in fact she does not seem to know quite what to do with the child. Cathy said 'Adam rang me from the airport. He said Valerie's ill in California. Why aren't you going?' I thought – I suppose because he wanted me to have the baby and then you could come and see it. I said 'I don't know.' She said 'Oh yes, he's clever.' She looked as if she might be about to cry.

I was thinking – But you must have always known you were going to look after the baby.

Cathy said 'I suppose he wanted you and I to talk, but I can see absolutely no point in talking, one just has to give in, surrender.' She put the baby back in its cot. She stood looking down on it. The room was getting dark. I thought – Even when it gets completely dark, I don't suppose she will talk.

She said 'I didn't want to bring a baby into this world. You knew that. What's the point of one more baby when the whole of humanity is longing for destruction? But Adam wanted it. And he couldn't have a baby. So why shouldn't he.'

'And here you are.'

'Oh you're all so clever! You think people change.'

'They go on journeys.'

'Who?'

'You.'

'When the baby was inside me I felt like an incubator. Eggs and chickens for human consumption.'

'You can stay here. Upstairs.'

'Would Valentina like that?'

'Yes.'

The baby was making a slight mewing noise. Cathy picked it up and held it again with her cheek against its head.

She said 'What about that girl you fucked just once and left.'

'What about her?'

'I want to have something to hold against you. You're so smug!'

'I suppose so.'

'Oh I know – then you saw me at the bus stop, and then you met Valentina.'

'Yes.'

'And now I'm here with the baby.' She laughed. 'God help us.' Then 'All right, I might stay here till Adam gets back. From being with his mother.'

'Yes you do that.'

'But I can't talk any more. You're right. We can't tell each other anything.'

'But we do.'

'Oh yes we do. And I'm grateful, you know that, don't you.'

'No I can't know that. Yes I mean I do.'

'Do you think I just wanted to come home?'

'Oh not just that. You can stay either in Valentina's bedroom or in Adam's old room.'

'The first time I met you we were talking about bedrooms.'

20

Adam rang me from California. He said 'Mum's all right.
Charlie Richtoven wants to come and see you.'

'He's already seen me.'

'He's got something new.'

'What was wrong with Mum?'

'She wants me to get her back to England.'

'Oh good.'

'Did Cathy come and see you?'

'Yes she's here now.'

'With the baby?'

'Yes.'

'Oh good.'

'What does Charlie want?'

'He seems to think the human race needn't be wiped out.
But it's got to learn a bit more about human nature.'

'Which is what?'

'Its drugs. Learn about its own brand of drugs.'

'Which is what it's doing.'

'No. I mean envy, resentment.'

'They're drugs?'

'Yes. To make life bearable. Nature's very cruel. Humans

believe they shouldn't be cruel, so they find justifications.'

'But don't we need to get off drugs?'

'Yes. But by knowing about them. Working with them. Not to be dominated by them. Is there anything in nature that isn't to some extent dependent on drugs?'

'You mean when they might be necessary and when not?'

'We might sometimes need nature's drugs to get off our own. Or vice versa.'

'You mean get off envy and resentment? But in order to learn, we should have access to drugs?'

'Perhaps to be able to choose when not to use them. Which we can't at the moment because they and information about them are kept in the hands of experts. Who don't look at evidence within themselves.'

'It's easier to blame others? To lay down the law for others?'

'There's something in the brain that doesn't want to grow up. Or wants to become moribund, stop functioning.'

'And not much in between?'

'It's a strain to include oneself being responsible.'

'But children can learn—'

'Until the world is too scornful of them.'

I thought – I suppose I am understanding this, but I don't know if my brain wants to hold it much.

But something will be taking it in somewhere?

Adam said 'I suppose Charlie thinks that people who get hooked on drugs can spend a lifetime getting off them. Something to do. People could do this about their other addictions.'

'But don't we?'

'Not our emotional addictions. We think them fun. Envy and resentment are the stuff of entertainment.'

'So what can we do—'

'Give up. Give oneself up.'

'But what to?'

'Oh there's that, yes. But as you say, one can't talk about it.'

Cathy had come into the room. She was carrying her baby. She pointed to herself and shook her head, as if indicating that she did not wish to speak to Adam.

I said 'How mad is Charlie?'

'Fairly. But he's read that madness is the mark of a creative mind. What distinguished the first human from apes.'

'Is that the latest?'

'Yes. But you can't go back to apes.'

'Nor on to robots.'

'But madness is too dangerous. It's not much fun any more.'

'But you can't inject yourself with sanity. Even if the experts say you can.'

'They might have done. But now they admit it's what's called a body-mind problem. Or a body-mind-environment problem. God help us.'

'You mean now they know they don't know what to do about it?'

'They can't say what to do about it. The individual has to find out for himself. Watch. Listen. Go on a journey.'

I thought – You mean it's a God problem.

Adam said 'Also Charlie thinks he's got a corner of the heroin trade that the Americans have liberated in Afghanistan. So there'll be plenty of chances to look at evidence.'

'Do the Americans know they've done that?'

'They know and they don't know. I mean they don't know they don't know. No wonder they can't talk about it.'

'People here say that they're working on a pill that will do away with guilt and conscience so that everyone in the armed forces will do just what they're told.'

'They've already got that. Haven't you noticed?'

'So anyone can be killed? No matter on whose side?'

'They call it a happiness pill.'

'Or suicide pill.'

Cathy said 'Is Valerie coming home?'

Adam said 'You can't tell people what to do in every situation because you don't know what every situation is. So people end up doing what they like.'

I said 'Evolution as an amusement arcade.'

Cathy said 'He's just a boring film producer.'

I said 'What?'

Adam said 'Is that Cathy?'

I said 'Charlie?'

I held the telephone out to Cathy but she shook her head.

Adam seemed to be talking to someone at the other end of the line.

I said into the telephone 'So it's not just an idea, a way of talking. It might have an effect?'

Adam said 'The brain being of the same stuff as the universe.'

Cathy said 'He's a story-teller. He thinks he can fix things like a film.'

I was thinking – This conversation might seem to be out of control because it is not aimed at being in control; but just because of this something unusual might emerge?

Adam said 'Is Cathy saying that Charlie's a boring American film producer?'

I said 'Yes.'

'Well so he was. He bought a studio a year ago. He was going to make a film.'

Cathy said 'You only like him because he didn't mind when you came back to see Valerie and stopped her having an abortion.'

I said 'It wasn't an abortion it was a hysterectomy.'

Adam said 'Mum's asking if you're drunk.'

I said 'No I'm thinking of giving up drink.'

Cathy said 'Why?'

I said 'As an experiment.'

Adam said 'Charlie wanted his film to be about what would happen if happiness or suicide pills were freely available.'

'And people wouldn't know the difference?'

'Well something unusual might happen. Charlie thinks that he might then be able to say he'd been supplying the armed forces with drugs.'

'Why?'

'Then they might not try to kill him.'

I thought – All right, this is not supposed to be rational.

Cathy said 'Did Valerie take an overdose?'

I said 'Did Valerie take an overdose?'

Adam said 'He was wanting to make this film.'

'And she wanted to show him?'

'Perhaps whatever it is wanted to show him.'

'Which is what. Show him what.'

Adam said 'I think that's why he wants to come and see you.' Then 'Ask Cathy how she thought she'd get funding for her project.'

Cathy said 'Tell Adam I love him.' Then she went out of the room, carrying her baby.

I said 'Cathy says will I tell you she loves you.'

Adam said 'Oh that, thank you, yes.'

I said 'And give my love to Valerie.'

Adam said 'I will.'

I rang off. I had not thought about ringing off. I had not asked Cathy how she thought she would get funding for her project. I did not know what Cathy's project was.

I thought I should get back, before it was too late, to my story of the two people, a Jew and a Christian, getting out of

185

Jerusalem. They had wanted to get away from the tribal addictions of being either Romans or Jews. They had come to the Dead Sea. They had to try to find a way across the Dead Sea. With inflatable body bags? Would that make a popular film?

But had I not already said that on their way to the Dead Sea they had picked up a baby? Which would or would not turn turtle? Was this before I had cottoned on about Cathy and Adam's baby?

Had I ever found out what was involved in turning turtle: would one end up looking at the sky?

I had to stop thinking.

By the time Valentina got back from her freebie in Scandinavia or Vienna or wherever it was she was dealing with ordinary human predicaments, Cathy and the baby had returned to the flat in south London that she had been sharing on and off with Adam. She had mentioned something, yes, about she and others possibly having a scheme ready to put before Adam when he returned—

I thought – 'Others' being not Charlie but the baby's alternative mothers?

When Valentina appeared I said 'I've missed you! I've needed you! I think I'm going mad! There is a theory that this is what differentiates us from humans!'

She said 'Don't you mean apes?'

'No, we know we're mad. It might be this that differentiates us from humans.'

'Just let me sit down.'

'Did you have a nice time?'

'You said Cathy's been here with the baby?'

'Oh yes, I tried to find you.'

'Do you think Adam ever intended to look after the baby?'

'Oh I'm sure. But it was also a good way for him to get Cathy.'

'Do you think he's carrying on with the au pair?'

'You mean he's actually got an au pair?'

'I told Cathy I'd pay for one.'

'No wonder they've been so cautious. Who is the au pair?'

'More like a mother's help. I think someone they picked up in Jerusalem.'

'Just let me lie down.'

I thought – I will lie on my back and look up at the sky.

When Charlie Richtoven came to see me for the second time it was as if he had no memory of the first; or rather, that this might be the second rehearsal of a play. He was wearing his dark glasses but the black man was not with him. I thought – Perhaps his story is that his security has been withdrawn so that someone or other can kill him.

He said 'Can I have a whisky?' I said 'Help yourself.' I propped myself up by the window as if I were not aware that I might be shot in the back.

He said 'When the Jews split with the Christians that was the end of the viability of the human race.'

I said 'That's old hat.'

'It's not too late.'

'Did Valerie take an overdose?'

'She wanted that cut.'

He sat down heavily in my armchair. He took off his dark glasses. It was as if he were blinded by light.

I said 'She's coming over here?'

He said 'She wanted a change without a reason.'

He seemed on the point of going to sleep. I thought – This is ridiculous! He's sitting in my armchair! He thinks he's taking over from me.

Then he opened his eyes and sat up. He said 'If it's not free will nor drugs, what is it? There should be a word.'

I said 'There was.'

'What was it?'

'Word.'

'Yes. But that's old hat.'

'Yes.'

'So what is it?'

'That. It doesn't stand for anything except itself.'

I thought – Well if it's not God, what is it.

He lay back and closed his eyes.

I began to think that I should get through on my mobile phone to Valentina who was upstairs and tell her that Charlie might be dying in my armchair. He might not know if he had taken a happiness or a suicide pill.

I went into the passage and got through to Valentina's answering machine upstairs. I said 'Darling Valentina, could you come down for a moment please? I think Charles von Richtoven may be dying in my armchair.'

Valentina's recorded voice said 'I am with a patient at the moment. Can you please leave a message?'

I said 'I might have left my message too early. I think I'm out of synch with these machines.'

I sat on the lowest step of the stairs. I thought – Why are patients called patients? Because they have to unlearn so many old techniques?

Valentina appeared at the top of the stairs. She said 'What makes you think Charlie Richtoven is dying in your armchair?'

I said 'Have a look.'

She climbed down over me and briefly looked into my room. Then she shut the door and said 'He doesn't look too bad.'

I said 'I think he's outed himself about supplying drugs to the American armed forces. He thinks they might kill him.'

'Well I suppose they might.'

'On the other hand, he may be able to say he was making a film.'

Valentina came and sat beside me on the stairs. She said 'But that's still playing games.'

I said 'Yes. But if it brings us together—'

'We've always been together!'

I put my arm awkwardly round her shoulders. 'Yes, but at the beginning—'

'Oh at a beginning!'

'All the same, do you think you could possibly go outside and see if there's a large black man lurking in the street or in the garden? I think he might be keeping an eye on Charlie.'

Valentina said 'This is schizophrenia!'

I said 'Yes, it's what distinguishes us from apes.'

Valentina went to the door into the garden and looked out. Then she came back and sat by me again. She said 'Now you've got me doing it.'

I said 'Darling Valentina, can I come up and sleep with you tonight?'

'Of course.'

'We can leave Charlie.'

'Have you got anything you mind about in your room?'

'Only my entire life's work on my computer.'

'Oh that, yes.'

'But look where it's getting me!'

'Can you make it up the stairs?'

21

The war in Iraq began and was said to have ended. There had not been many American and British casualties, and a high proportion of these had been caused by so-called friendly fire. Casualties were large among Iraqi civilians, and hospitals that might have treated them had been bombed. The reason for going to war was said to have been the existence of Iraqi weapons of mass destruction, but no such weapons were found. In the months after the so-called liberation more American soldiers were killed in guerrilla attacks than during the war: the headquarters of the United Nations and the International Red Cross were blown up, and staff had to be withdrawn. For the rebuilding of Iraq it had been intended that contracts would be given to American companies and profits would be ensured by the sale of Iraqi oil. But none of this seemed to be happening.

An air of satisfied bafflement settled down over those who had been in favour of war: they could be said to have won; they had kept their money and their jobs. And why should it not be acceptable that the situation should settle into a programme of unlawful detentions and tit-for-tat killings such as Cathy had reported as being the status quo in

Bethlehem? There need not be official approval or disapproval: people were at home in a condition conducive to perpetual complaint. And it could be argued earnestly that this was better than a society succeeding in heroic purpose.

I would have liked to have said to Charlie Richtoven – Your policy of spreading senseless information seems to work: bafflement is healthier than arrogance or despair.

But Charlie had disappeared – both from my basement during the night, and from the orbit of anyone who might be expected to know where he was. He had left in my room small packets of his happiness or suicide pills: their effect would be, yes, that only by taking them would you find out which they were.

I was rung up by my old friend Tom who was now vice-chancellor of a provincial university. Since I had seen him at the Hendersons' dinner I had imagined him as at least a part-time member of MI5. He said 'Valerie's friend von Richtoven has been put on a hit-list by the Israelis. This is after his company has announced it has discovered a cure for schizophrenia.'

I said 'You mean there's a connection? The Israelis are dependent on their need to feel persecuted?'

'Ah it's good to talk to you. I knew you'd see the joke!'

'All fundamentalists are schizophrenic. But what had Charlie been saying?'

'That of course everyone should accept the strict rabbinical tradition, which says that the state of Israel should extend right up to the Euphrates.'

'Isn't that up by Baghdad?'

'Yes. And Charlie says that because the Jews are the only people who claim that God promised them a particular piece of land, people of other religions should accept this, especially Islamists, who have been told that their faith has nothing to do with land, that it is an other-worldly religion. So the Islamists have got it in for Charlie too.'

'Yes, that's quite witty.'

'No one likes others to take their religion seriously.'

'Charlie was here the other day.'

'So you'd better watch out.'

'He's disappeared. His aim is to make us admit we're absurd. Then this might distinguish us from humans.'

'Yes, that's witty.'

'Charlie thinks God is witty.'

'Anyway he's become something of a pariah in the Middle East, I mean Charlie, but something of a hero to the Americans, who think anyone who has a cure for anything is a god, but especially one advocating Israel getting control of all the troublesome land up to the Euphrates.'

'But what's his cure for schizophrenia?'

'Something about redistribution of fat in the brain. It's that which distinguishes us from apes.'

'Yes—'

'And buttocks and breasts. And you know how fat Americans are.'

'But you mean fat's a good thing? In brains and buttocks and breasts?'

'But that's the snag. Humans find it difficult to distinguish between buttocks and breasts and brains.'

'And that's a bad thing?'

'I don't know.'

'Dear Tom, it's a wonder to be talking to you again.'

Tom said 'You can get it on the Net.'

So after we had rung off I got out my laptop computer and set about remembering how to get on to the Net. There had been a time when I had used it a lot to look for facts and theories, but I had come to see it as a purveyor of information as likely to be untrue as true; and with no means of telling the difference. So was it mainly useful in Charlie's sense of making an uncertainty of everything – perhaps with the exception of its voluminous portrayals of buttocks and breasts. But I had forgotten my password to enter this fairy realm. A password had no meaning except as a trick. You clicked and interminable advertisements came up – some both encouraging and discouraging fatness, yes.

I eventually came to an account of the latest theory about schizophrenia. It was an illness, yes; but it had also been a blessing, because it represented what distinguished humans from their closest relations, chimpanzees. At a point in history there had been a mutation in the brain of a single hominoid ancestor – the chance secretion or distribution of a certain fatty acid – and this had given to the hominoid the impression that there was more to life than just what he or she could touch, taste, hear, see, smell; more even than the fine examples of fat that were lying in wait for him somewhere on the Net – the monstrous buttocks and breasts. (This was my own wearying witticism.) There was order, meaning, beauty, holiness; personified perhaps by gods and goddesses who would be represented often enough in works of art by – yes you've got it. But all this did seem to be beyond the range of animals who were saddled with touch, taste, sight, sound, smell; but then so, still, were humans; with just the addition of order, meaning, beauty, holiness, as well as – all right! No wonder they could not avoid madness—

—except by some further disposition of fat, preferably in the brain?

Or wherever it is that stories exist.

So in order to divert my own incipient madness I thought I would go out into our small front garden and sit in the autumn sun.

There was a collapsible garden chair that was kept in the basement passage. I could drag this without too much difficulty up the garden steps; then I might at least be out in the open if hit-men came looking for Charlie or myself – but no, no, not this sort of story. At least I was able now to see this as a boring story.

I dragged the collapsible chair onto the paving in the garden. There was trellis-work with creepers that protected the garden from the street. I set the chair up beside the central feature of the garden which was a cypress tree in a tub. I thought – Now here is order and beauty; a secret enclave in the town: this is the sort of thing that Adam and Eve must have hoped to create for themselves after God had lost his cool and behaved to them so disgracefully: this would not be a bad story? How long was it before God had visited them after he'd turned them out of the Garden? Had it been their fault? Should they have been more entertaining? Something more, surely, could be made of this story! Then when I sat on the chair it collapsed underneath me, trapping my bad leg between the metal of the seat and the metal of its stand, with my enormous weight on top of it. I wondered if my leg might be broken again. The last time I had been given morphine. I could surely do with some morphine now, but Charlie's suicide pills were in the house. This was a situation humans had been told to dread – to be in hell and to have left it too late to get out. So was there a case for even toddlers to be equipped with personal suicide pills so as not to be caught out— Sorry, God, I said I'd make no more such jokes. But what if it was after all a happiness pill? I was propping myself with an arm behind me on the ground and thus raising myself slightly so that I was in some semi-lotus position with one leg folded underneath me. Should I then meditate? I was not in much pain. The pain would come later when the terrorists came in with their baseball bats— Sorry, sorry! but jokes are what humans have been good at. I pushed against the chair with my free hand so that I might even levitate, but the jaws of the mantrap just tightened round me. And could I not even make a face which might be like that of a martyr being burned at the stake? Then I tried pulling on the tub but it seemed about to topple on top of me. So I thought I'd better stay still. But supposing there had been the ultimate terrorist attack and there was no one else left on earth – All right, then it's up to you, God. I could not remember what time Valentina had said she would be home. But I was once more spending nights with her! So wasn't I lucky. And what if I am like a tick hanging from a twig spending an eternity waiting for some animal to pass beneath it so it can fall on to it and burrow beneath its skin and thus survive—

There was someone coming through the gate from the street onto the path through the garden that led to the front door and that of the basement. But indeed no more jokes! A figure came into view – of a woman tip-toeing quietly. She did not go to either of the doors but came round in front of the cypress tree to where she could look in through the basement window. She was so intent on what she was doing that she did not see me behind her by the tub where I was sitting like a buddha. I said to myself – Nadia? She was older, of course, but not so different. I did not want to make a sound to distract her from my being able to watch her. She had her back to me and was leaning forwards to look through the window. She wore a denim skirt and flat-heeled shoes and had bare legs. I was thinking – She has the same sort of effect on me as the Taj Mahal.

After a time she turned and said 'I could see your reflection in the window. It was as if you were both in your room and out here.'

I said 'I thought I should come out into the garden.'

'I might not have had the courage to ring your bell.'

'Oh of course you would!'

'But I knew which was your room.'

She came and knelt down by me. She was something that I could taste, touch, smell. But I could not put an arm around her because the complex position I was in might collapse and I might lose my leg: but how lucky I was not to have lost it the first time so that I could now be trapped! I said 'How did you know which was my room?' She said 'I'd have tapped at your window.' She put an arm round my shoulders.

She was trying to stand and lift me all at once. I took my hand away from the ground and put both arms around her and then it was as if we were in free-fall with only one parachute. She said 'I thought it might be difficult seeing you.' I said 'And now it's not.' She lifted me, and my leg came clear of the chair and I kicked it away and it fell like the used component of a rocket. I thought – What is the word, oh yes, that is the opposite of deposition?

Valentina appeared in the garden. She was carrying shopping bags in her Aquarius-the-water-carrier role. She said 'What on earth are you doing out here?' I said 'We're just coming in.' Valentina said 'Can you manage?' Nadia said 'Yes I think so.' Valentina said 'I'll go ahead and make some tea.'

22

Nadia and I sat in Valentina's drawing room while Valentina
was in the kitchen. I thought – Nadia could be a daughter-
in-law or stepdaughter? I said 'Have you ever been back to
your family?'

'No, I don't think they would have wanted it.'

'They needed you to stay clear—'

'They're very practical.'

I was thinking – We're still like the same poles of magnets:
how could we have stayed together!

I said 'So what have you been doing? Barbara didn't tell me
much.'

'I've been a teacher.'

'What do you teach?'

'English. Literature. What I studied at the university you
took me to.'

'You got your degree?'

'Yes.'

'I knew little of this.'

'You didn't want to. I was teaching in Jerusalem when I
met Cathy.'

'You met Cathy?'

'You think that unlikely? I was at a school for Palestinians. I speak Arabic.'

'Of course.'

'I wanted to tell them how to live in a hostile world. You should both expect and not expect people to be hostile.'

Valentina came in with tea things. She set down the tray. I said 'Nadia knew Cathy in Jerusalem.'

Valentina said 'I don't think I can bear to hear much more about Cathy in Jerusalem just at the moment.' She went out.

Nadia said 'I told my pupils that I came from a land that was thought to have been the Garden of Eden. We knew what it was to have been turned out.' She laughed.

'And what did they say?'

'They laughed.'

'What else?'

'I told them I had been tricked by someone who thought he was God. So of course I had to get out.'

'And did they laugh?'

'No. But I think they thought I was trying to be funny.'

She drank her tea. I tried to imagine what it would be like now to make love to Nadia. My mind slowed and stopped.

I said 'I didn't know at the time the story of why you had to get out.'

'Barbara has told you? Do you think I was deceiving you?'

'No not at all.'

'I told myself I wanted you to be helping me not because it was charitable but because you needed to. Do you think that was right?'

'Yes I think that was right.'

Nadia looked very tired. I wondered where she had been living. She said 'I wanted to be trusted. Can trust only happen if you're not sure what things are?'

'I suppose so, yes.' Then 'I didn't behave well.'

'How could you have behaved better? You saved my life. Sparked it on course. At the cost of yours.'

'No.'

There was another silence. I wondered – Did those people who wanted to get up to heaven ever get any words out?

Valentina put her head round the door. She looked from one to the other of us. She said 'I'm just going out for a walk, is that all right?'

Nadia said 'Yes.' Valentina went out.

I said 'When you met Cathy did you tell her who you were?'

Nadia said 'No, I didn't know who she was. Then they were talking about this person who had had the idea that one should risk everything for an impossible love if one wanted to learn that one didn't yet know what things are. And I said that this idea came from one of our poems.'

'And what did they say?'

'There was talk about what was an impossible love.'

'And what did you say?'

'That that wasn't the point. That you risk things for what seems necessary.'

'And what did Cathy say?'

'How do you know what is necessary.'

'And what did Tania say?'

'Oh yes you knew Tania, didn't you?'

'It was you I didn't know.'

'Perhaps that wasn't necessary. They guessed at some point that I had known you. But this was so unlikely that they didn't want to ask. I mean we'd all come together because we wanted to do something about Bethlehem and Jerusalem.'

'And then the baby.'

'Yes.'

'So there was no need to talk about me.'

'You can't talk about that sort of thing, don't you say?'

I thought – You make me sound like that impossible old God.

I said 'But what did Tania say?'

'Oh well, Tania said she didn't see why the sort of love we had been talking about had to be impossible. If the point of it was to make you humble, then surely you could be humbled if you got what you wanted at the same time. And Cathy said – Oh yes, she'd heard that sort of thing from someone before.'

I thought – Valentina used to tell me how lucky I was with Cathy.

I said 'And did you know at the time about Cathy having a baby?'

'We knew she was pregnant. What I wanted at the time was just for Tania to use her influence with the Israelis to take us all in her truck on an expedition to the Dead Sea.'

'The Dead Sea!'

'Tania could get to places other people couldn't because she was in television. We all felt we had to get away from Bethlehem and Jerusalem for a time.'

'But why the Dead Sea?'

'I wanted to snorkel. I wondered if I might see the ruins of Sodom and Gomorrah on the bottom. But people said one couldn't snorkel in the Dead Sea.'

'Why not?'

'Because it's too salty. You flip over onto your back.'

'That's just what I wanted to know!'

'Why?'

'I've been writing a story about two people going to the Dead Sea. One's an orthodox Jew and the other's a born-again Christian. They're both obsessed with the story of Sodom and Gomorrah because if it's true that religion's a matter of rules and regulations, then there's damnation for anyone who breaks them, which everyone does.'

'Did Cathy know about your story?'

'No, I don't think so.'

'That's what fundamentalist Muslims think too.'

'So did Cathy go to the Dead Sea? Did she want to?'

'She didn't want to bring a baby into the same old world. She wanted something new.'

'She hadn't had the baby yet?'

'She was still wondering what to do. She had wanted to have it for Adam.'

'Why?'

'I think she thought it was just something about which Adam might be able to do something new.'

'Better than her?'

'But I think she thought she'd find out something if she went to the Dead Sea. I mean this was a picture she had – of an enormous warm bath where you could have babies without too much pain and so you wouldn't be perpetuating pain on to your children. And if you were haunted by the story of Sodom and Gomorrah, then you might be flipped over and look at the sky.'

I stared at Nadia. She stared back at me. I thought – You mean, even if it didn't happen exactly like that, it's true.

I said 'Go on.'

'Well we were staying in a village in an old Essene encampment. There was an Israeli checkpoint nearby on the road. We'd been talking about what to do when the time came for Cathy to have her baby – the Israelis were being tough with protesters like Cathy, who were basically trying to protect Palestinians. They'd shot and wounded one of Cathy's people when they were trying to cross Manger Square. The Israelis could take Cathy into custody any time, and take the baby. We'd been talking about how it might be best when the time came for Tania to say it was her baby: she had all this influence because she'd been carrying on with the Israeli commander in Bethlehem.'

I said 'But are you saying that Cathy had her baby actually in the Dead Sea? Or by the Dead Sea? Or whatever?'

'In or by that uniquely salubrious and saliferous environment: or in the Essene village: or at the Israeli command post with an ambulance ready to rush her to hospital in Jerusalem.'

I thought – You mean, you can choose your story?

Nadia said 'Each or none of those things. What does it matter.'

'But she did have the baby.'

'Oh yes.'

'And Tania and her Israeli could fix things?'

'He said he'd do anything so long as he wasn't thought to be the father.'

'But could Tania be thought to be the mother? Was that possible?'

'The situation was very chaotic. No one was trying to tell or know the truth at the time. If it had fitted, I could have said that the baby was mine, because I'd been with a nice Palestinian boy. But that could hardly have helped in the practical situation.'

'So the baby could have three possible mothers – one the girlfriend of a Jew, one the girlfriend of a Palestinian, and one—'

'For a time I even wondered if you might be the father. But no, not really! You were so evidently that impossible and unpredictable old Daddy-God who'd got us all into this predicament, impregnated us as it were, then left us to get free again. For which we were all unspeakably grateful!' She laughed.

I thought I heard Valentina coming back into the house. I said 'But what was Adam doing all this time?'

'He was said to be working for someone trying to corner

the drug market somewhere – Afghanistan I think – but whether to exploit it or close it down wasn't clear. But you must know about that? Adam didn't turn up in Palestine till after Cathy had had the baby. He said he hadn't wanted to put pressure on anyone, which sounded false, but he knew that, and so it wasn't. And he said he'd be glad to adopt the baby if that was how things turned out.'

'And what did you make of that?'

'I didn't. Something, yes, was being worked out.'

'There must be some point in men not being able to have babies—'

'But then turning up when there's something to be sorted out.'

Nadia lay back on her chair. She looked as if she were struggling with sleep.

I said 'But people in those poems of yours are always moving on. They avoid the tentacles reaching up from Sodom and Gomorrah.'

Nadia said 'And they get sustenance from the sky as they flip over onto their backs halfway across the Dead Sea.'

'But Sufis are wanderers. They don't have children.'

'But you've always wanted the best of both worlds, haven't you?'

I thought – I too will soon become incapacitated by sleep. But we may never be able to talk like this again. I said 'Just one more thing. Is it true you once killed a man who was trying to rape you?'

'That's what Barbara told you?'

'Yes.'

'When?'

'Just the other day.'

'And you really didn't mind I hadn't told you?'

'No.'

'Well they did need to get me out of the country, yes. But it wasn't quite like that.'

I thought – But don't let Nadia be all too ordinarily human!

She said 'He was a holy man, a mullah, who had been teaching me Islamic law. I could see that I troubled him. He said he wished to watch while I make love with one of his servant boys: he said unfortunately he was not able to do it himself. He said he knew I was interested in the boy because he had been watching me, and this was true in a way, because the boy was beautiful. But my teacher said that if I ever told anyone of what he had suggested, or if I refused, he would say that he had come across the two of us making love and then the boy would be flogged and I would be stoned or whatever according to law. But there were stories about this sort of thing before, weren't there? So I thought he would probably say he had come across us anyway, even if I did what he wanted, because he would always be frightened of what I might say. And so I told him that I was sure he could manage it himself, and I set about him, and he got excited, and then he had a sort of fit. And his people came in and saw him on top of me with my clothes torn, and then later he apparently tried to kill himself with a knife. Or that was what they said. But really no one knew what to make of the story.'

I said 'Is that ending true?'

'Do you think it would be better if he'd tried to rape me and I'd killed him?'

I said 'No, not really.'

Valentina put her head round the door. She said 'Are you two decent?'

Nadia said 'No, not really.' She laughed.

Valentina said 'Would anyone like a drink?'

Nadia said 'Yes please.'

I said 'We've been talking about how does one make words represent what's true.'

Valentina said 'And what have you decided. Red or white?'

Nadia said 'Red please.'

I said 'One seldom sees or knows what actually happens, as there are too many things going on all at once. And truth depends on the context of the whole set-up anyway – not only where it's come from but especially where it might be going.'

Valentina said 'He sometimes goes on like this for hours.' Nadia laughed.

I said 'But still, it's an interesting problem, so why can't people talk about it?'

Valentina said 'Because it's not witty.' She smiled, and handed a glass of wine to Nadia.

Nadia said 'What I came to tell you was that Adam and Cathy are setting up a sort of caravanserai, or staging-post, where people can bring their children, or stay, if they want to.'

Valentina said 'But they won't be allowed.'

'Then they'll have tried it, and people can move on.'

I said 'Is that what Charlie Richtoven's supposed to be putting up money for?'

Nadia said 'I don't think Cathy wanted that.'

Valentina said 'And I forgot to tell you that Adam's bringing Valerie here in the morning. Their flight gets in early.' She was watching Nadia, who appeared to be falling asleep again.

I said 'Where is this place? What's happened to Charlie?'

Valentina said 'I thought you said he's trying out his cure for schizophrenia.'

I said 'Well it seems to be working.'

Valentina said 'She can sleep here.'

23

When Adam and Valerie arrived in the early morning Valerie was in a wheelchair and looked exhausted. I thought – But I was the one who was dying! I bent to give her a kiss on the cheek in the manner to which we had been accustomed and not for the first time my foot slipped and I toppled with my arms on either side of her. Adam said 'Oi oi!' Valentina said to Valerie 'Are you all right?' Valerie said 'Yes I'm only in this chair because it's so useful to be disabled.' Adam said 'But do be taken in by that.' I got myself upright and we went through the garden and up the steps to the main part of the house. Adam said to Nadia 'You say they might be coming this morning to knock it down?' Nadia said 'You see, they're taking notice.' Adam said 'Well it'll save us a lot of trouble.' The driver of the car in which Adam and Valerie had come from the airport was the black man Charlie; he came to help Adam manoeuvre the wheelchair up the steps. I said 'Hello Charlie, do you know where the other Mr Charlie is?' He said 'He's taking a bit of a sabbatical, Mr Valentina.' I wondered – With false ringlets and a beard? Valentina said 'Who wants breakfast.'

There had been announcements on the early morning

news of more suicide bombings: what seemed to make these newsworthy was only whether the numbers were slightly up or down. I said to Adam 'Cathy and the baby stayed for three days.' Adam said 'That should do the trick.' Valentina said 'Aren't you going to give her a name?' Adam said 'Oh yes, one will turn up.'

We had breakfast of boiled eggs and toast and coffee. The driver Charlie said he would prefer tea, which Valentina made for him. Adam said he wouldn't sit down because he was afraid if he did he'd fall asleep. I thought – We have managed to land on the far side of the Dead Sea?

We went out to the car and Adam and Nadia helped Valerie onto the back seat; Charlie folded the chair and put it in the boot. I held the door open for Valentina so that she could sit by Valerie; but she hung back: Adam said 'It's absolutely vital that you be there.' So Valentina climbed in, and Nadia sat in the front by Charlie, and Adam and I were on the two small seats in the back facing Valerie and Valentina. I thought – There is now such field-force or whatever it is called between us that there might be some aurora borealis in the desert?

We drove to the river and then across it. I felt – We are in a funeral cortège of spirits about to be liberated. I was trying to avoid catching the eye of Valentina or Valerie as this might spark off a chain reaction of laughter. In Nadia's village people had not liked to look at each other directly because this might invoke the evil eye. I thought – But that was a false evil.

I remembered Adam mentioning a property in a derelict area south of the river that he had hoped to acquire and, yes, turn it into something like what Nadia had called a caravanserai. Here people could come and go and bring or leave children in the course of whatever so-called journey they might be on. This could have been a metaphor? But what do you go on a journey for?

We drove under a railway viaduct into, yes, a desolate ex-dockland area of dismantled railway sidings and rubble. Beyond this there were two tall tower blocks of what must have been council flats but which now themselves seemed derelict – or possibly homes for squatters. Yes, there were ghostly figures beyond half-boarded up windows. Around the tower blocks was an area which might have been designed as a garden or perhaps allotments but now was a dump for abandoned cars. On wasteland between this and ourselves an effort had been made to clear a football pitch: there were elegant goalposts at one end and at the other end two piles of oil drums. At the side nearest to where we had come in there was a building with a low sloping roof with planks propped along it so that they were like seating on the upper tier of a grandstand. At one end of the building there was a tower with its top knocked off which might once have been part of a church or a chapel. There was a door into this with above it a board like a shop-sign hanging crookedly; on it were the words WILLIES EMPORIUM. Adam said 'I know it should have an apostrophe.' Valerie said 'How did you find this place?' Adam said 'We sort of came across it.'

Valentina said 'Did you have to make the football pitch or was it already here?'

Adam said 'It fitted in quite nicely.'

Nadia said 'It needs a few trees.'

I said 'They'd do better for a cricket field.'

Valentina said 'You can buy almost fully grown palm trees.'

Valerie said 'They need awfully big holes.'

Adam said 'Which people can jump into and climb out of.'

I seemed to remember (or was this what the scene led me to imagine?) that Adam's building had once been a non-conformist chapel which had been damaged by bombing in 1940; it had been earmarked to be pulled down, but a preservation order had been placed on it on the grounds that it was of historical interest, being representative of dockland life. So then it had become a shop selling bric-a-brac. Adam had been offered a lease on it on condition that he carried out repairs. Or was it that Charlie had bought the site as a speculative investment?

The car went round to the far side of the building where there was a larger door with another board propped on its end beside it saying in gothic lettering CHAPEL OF REST. The driver Charlie got out of the car and lifted the wheelchair from the boot; Adam picked up the notice saying CHAPEL OF REST and propped it horizontally on the bonnet of the car against the windscreen. He said 'We thought it might put people off nicking the tyres.' I said 'And did it?' Adam said 'We also thought of leaving a length of hose-pipe on the front seat so that people could gas themselves if they wanted to.' I thought of saying – Did you remember to leave the car keys? I got out of the car: I was beginning to feel dizzy, with a tight band of pain around my chest. I thought – Perhaps after all I am dying! I had become so accustomed to saying that one got ill for a purpose rather than from a cause that I thought I might look to see whether in fact they had left the keys.

Nadia had taken over the chair from Charlie and was pushing Valerie into the building. I still did not want to catch Valentina's eye; especially if I were not going to joke about my prospective fatal heart attack. I followed Valerie and Nadia into the large interior space that was more like that of a mosque than a church or a chapel; there were no pews nor chairs but a mass of rugs and cushions on the floor: these were threadbare as if they had been taken from a rubbish skip and scrubbed and scraped meticulously clean. Against the wall opposite the door were poles and boards of scaffolding up to the ceiling; this gave the impression that a fresco was about to be created or cleaned. At the far end of the large space were a few children of various ages sitting or crawling on the floor; they were surrounded by what appeared to be the contents of a tip for old electrical appliances – or a modern work of art. The children were moving amongst these bits and pieces gravely playing or experimenting with them; reassembling them where they would fit, or fashioning them into new conjunctions. Nadia left Valerie and went to the children and bent down and spoke to one or two; it seemed they were familiar enough with her not to pay much attention.

When Valerie had seen the scaffolding she had begun to push herself out of her chair as if in response to a call of nature. Adam offered her his arm and they went to the base of the scaffolding. I found a cushion which was more substantial than most and I pushed it with my sticks to the wall next to the scaffolding; I lowered myself onto it, or rather crash-landed, and then I got myself propped with my head and shoulders against the wall. I thought – Now I am looking at the sky!

Cathy was standing at the far end of the room with her baby, holding it with her cheek against its head. This was the style in which people seldom posed for paintings of the Virgin Mary. Cathy was in the middle of the bits and pieces of junk or art on the floor; she seemed to be looking for somewhere to put down her baby. There was an old-fashioned playpen of which one side was collapsed; she tried propping the baby in one corner where it might see what was going on but should not feel trapped. Cathy stood for a while as if to see also that it did not feel abandoned. I thought – The baby will be sorting out, shaping in its mind, what is happening.

Adam had helped Valerie up onto the first platform of the scaffolding where she was able to crawl on her own. Adam handed up to her a bag which he had carried from the car, which I recognised as one in which she used to carry her paints. Valerie took it and swung it up onto a higher platform and then used her hands as well as her feet to climb up after it.

At the far end of the room Nadia had gone to some lighting equipment such as is used by professional photographers – a lamp on a stand and a large reflector and screen of the kind that diffuses light when a lamp is shone on it. Nadia was setting up the reflector but was having difficulty in aligning it with the screen: Cathy moved as if to help her but then the baby became restless and Cathy stopped: Valentina had come into the interior carrying a bag that looked as if it contained provisions; she put the bag down and went up to Cathy and they embraced. The baby gazed beyond them impassively, in the way that babies do in pictures of the Adoration of the Magi. Cathy left Valentina and went to where Nadia was setting up the photographic equipment. Valentina picked up the baby and held it with her cheek against its head.

I was lying on my side on my cushion. The thought came to me that I might have already died – even as a result perhaps of having been hit by the van or juggernaut in New York – and all that had happened since then was what might have been seen from the very top of the mountain of purgatory.

Valerie had reached the top level of the scaffolding and had dragged up her painting equipment after her. Adam had gone to the door and was observing some disturbance that was going on just outside. I was thinking – But Valerie will not actually be painting the scene: she will be trying to capture the energy at the back of what is happening.

A bright light came on where Cathy and Nadia were working the photographic equipment. This illumined not the whole of the interior but particularly the door opposite the scaffolding where people who had been outside were now coming in. The scaffolding and the wall where I was sitting were left largely in the dark. At the door there was a woman coming in backwards with a professional video camera on her shoulder: I recognised Tania: she was filming the group of people who were entering after her and who were lit brightly by the equipment directed at them by Cathy and Nadia. This made them stop. They held their hands in front of their eyes. They looked awkward, or trying to be charming, as people are who are being photographed. Adam, with his back to the light, was facing them and was holding a hand out to them – whether to welcome them or ward them off was not clear. The people who had come in looked like bureaucrats or officials: it did not seem they could have any other function. I imagined – They have come to say that the building cannot be used because it has not been authorised, or is unsafe; or is going to be pulled down. Perhaps Adam had never had a lease on the building; in conjunction with people in the high-rise blocks he had been squatting. And Tania is filming the scene so that anyone who wishes will be able to see it as—

—an exercise, a demonstration, of how things are; of what is true but cannot last; of what is produced by the mind as an everlasting possibility. This is different from the way things work; in which things are built, have to be pulled down, to start again: this other is a style in which things can happen all at once, which can offer meaning. This can be seen from the dark – the children playing with artwork on the floor, Valerie overlooking the scene from a platform of scaffolding, Cathy and Nadia directing bright lights, Tania diverting the invaders by filming. And the baby having been held by both Cathy and Valentina now finding Cathy coming back to take it. And Adam lowering his hand and just watching the people at the door. And they seeming to be daunted. And Valentina coming and sitting by me on the cushion.

Valentina said 'Are you all right?'

I said 'I'm not sure.'

Tania stopped filming and put her camera down. There was a further commotion outside – the clanking sounds of bulldozers and of those machines which swing balls on the ends of chains like meteors and knock down walls. But they cannot knock down what is not contained by walls; which can form patterns in and apart from the brain.

There were more people coming in at the door: these were women, mostly young, with occasionally a man in tow. I thought – These are the squatters from the high-rise blocks: they have left their babies here as an experiment: they have now heard the bulldozers and have come to pick up their babies. They pushed past the people whom Adam had confronted at the door and they went to where the children were playing among the bits and pieces; they looked among them as if to discover their own. I thought – Perhaps they have not done this before: perhaps they will now set off on their journeys. They carried their children to where Cathy was now standing by Adam and was holding her baby in front of her like a cross on a shield: they gathered round her. I thought – They may learn not only to survive, but what to survive for.

Valentina was saying 'How are you feeling?'

I said 'I think I'm dying.'

She might once have said – You always think you're dying.

She said 'We'll get you to a doctor.'

I was trying to remember what had happened in New York. I had thought I saw someone I recognised at the far side of the road. Was it more likely to have been a stranger? An ambulance man had said 'By rights he should be dead.' Words had come into my mind – Things fall by the force of gravity: God is the force of levity. Was this witty? Perhaps the bulldozers were already doing their work; bits and pieces of skyscrapers landing on my head. What happens to you when you die: can you leapfrog over rights if there is enough levity?

Adam and Cathy were leaning over me. They held their

baby. The baby was like a cherub in the sky. Adam was saying 'What's wrong?' Valentina said 'He's feeling funny.' I said 'I think your baby's dropped a blob of spittle on my head.'

About the Author

Born in London on June 25, 1923, Nicholas Mosley was educated at Eton and Oxford. He served in Italy during World War II, and published his first novel, *Spaces of the Dark*, in 1951. Since then, he has published sixteen works of fiction, including the novels *Accident*, *Impossible Object*, and *Hopeful Monsters*, winner of the 1990 Whitbread Award. Mosley is also the author of several works of nonfiction, most notably the autobiography *Efforts at Truth* and a biography of his father, Sir Oswald Mosley, entitled *Rules of the Game/Beyond the Pale*. He currently resides in London, where he is at work on a nonfiction study of war and peace.

Coleman Dowell Series

The Coleman Dowell Series is made possible through a generous contribution by an anonymous donor. This endowed contribution allows Dalkey Archive Press to publish one book a year in this series.

Born in Kentucky in 1925, Coleman Dowell moved to New York in 1950 to work in theater and television as a playwright and composer/lyricist, but by age forty turned to writing fiction. His works include *One of the Children Is Crying* (1968), *Mrs. October Was Here* (1974), *Island People* (1976), *Too Much Flesh and Jabez* (1977), and *White on Black on White* (1983). After his death in 1985, *The Houses of Children: Collected Stories* was published in 1987, and his memoir about his theatrical years, *A Star-Bright Lie*, was published in 1993.

Since his death, a number of his books have been reissued in the United States, as well as translated for publication in other countries.

SELECTED DALKEY ARCHIVE PAPERBACKS

FOR A FULL LIST OF PUBLICATIONS, VISIT:
www.dalkeyarchive.com

SELECTED DALKEY ARCHIVE PAPERBACKS

FOR A FULL LIST OF PUBLICATIONS, VISIT:
www.dalkeyarchive.com